Hello Planet Earth

Adventure * Discover * Return

A Tale of True Life Myth and Fantasy

Michael Wallace

Ladder to the Moon Publications

Hello Planet Earth

Copyright © 2015 Michael Wallace

All Rights Reserved

Published by Ladder to the Moon Publications.
ISBN: 978-0-9756994-9-2
Mailing: PO Box 1355 Kingscliff, NSW 2487
WEB: www.laddertothemoon.com.au

You have to leave the city of your comfort
and go into the wilderness of your intuition.
What you'll discover will be wonderful.

What you'll discover is yourself.

Alan Alda

Other Books by this author:

The Book of Number Series

Jermimiah Versus the Grabblesnatch

The Divinity Dice Series

Ratology: Way of the Un-Dammed

Fragments of the Mirror

Water: More Precious than Gold

The Borringbar War

Hello Planet Earth

© Michael Wallace 1982. Revised 2015

IBSN: 978-0-9756994-9-2

Publisher: Ladder to the Moon

Web: laddertothemoon.com.au

INDEX

"There came a time when the risk to
remain tight in the bud was more painful
than the risk it took to blossom."

Anaïs Nin

It Started with a Sigh …

The Beginning

We shall not cease from exploration
And the end of all our exploring
Will be to arrive where we started
And to know the place for the first time
Through the unknown, remembered gate

T S Eliot

This whole business started with a sigh. A deep, long, disconsolate sigh. A sigh that hid many things inside. We see this often, though few notice. I learned to sigh quite early.

I was but 3 years of age, and visitors would come to the rather exotic house where the family lived, full of carving from the Sepic River, and that odd family from the highlands of New Guinea. The guests would ask where each of we children where we came from: Rabaul (They nod with interest) Port Moresby (Yes, most interesting) Manus Island (Very nice) Lae (Fascinating) Goroka (Wonderful coffee there I hear) and finally to myself, the youngest. "Brisbane" I would say, and as usual, the face on the visitor said quite clearly "Oh, dull".

I would sigh. WHY couldn't I have been born somewhere that was interesting? I felt so drab.

We all have a hidden dream. The woman gazing out to sea, looking at some far horizon: Who knows what heart-felt thoughts are running through her mind. An old man, looking at a photo album of his departed wife. A mother looking at her young child at play. Even a lonely dog waiting for the ball to be thrown, but his master is too drunk and has fallen asleep. At least they had lost a dream. I had never found one.

Maybe tomorrow it will change? We find ourselves in our personal Garden of Gethsemane, waiting for our hoped for messiah, yet we fall asleep in the humdrum slowness of our lives. We all want something important to occur, yet so few of us ever find this. We survive this sad realization by letting go of the pain with a sigh.

Who can capture in words the sense of this moment, the letting go of our disappointment that brings about such a release? It is a freeing from concern. A sigh is a message to the world that we are indifferent to its cruelty, even as we suffer it. It's a powerful thing that we possess, you and I. We all have it within us, this power to breath slowly outwards.

And many years later, at work, once more I sigh.

"John, we need some more cups for the coffee machine. Can you trot up to the storage and get some for us?" "John, we need some pins. Can you find us some pins somewhere?" And so it went every day.

I would sigh to myself, and do as I was asked. Who wouldn't sigh? I was a dogs body. People kept asking to do odd jobs that were just mindless and meaningless. Everything I did simply affirmed my sense of being utterly pointless. A sigh was a positive response, given the circumstances. Of course, the real issue was that I didn't really fit in. No one said anything, or made a comment, but I could tell. While my coworkers remained polite, I knew they all thought me a little strange.

Maybe it was the card tricks? Making cards appear and disappear, sitting at my desk, practicing magic, and generally imagining I had an audience to perform to.

Strange, you think? Perhaps, but the truth was that I was simply elsewhere. My thoughts at work were always more towards the weekend where I would do something more interesting than my present moment.

No one can blame the mere worker-ant who is given dull jobs for wandering away in their thoughts. But on this day I was simply not there.

At that point in time I was a mere minion, an office flunkey doing the bidding of the various bosses that had control of my 9 to 5 destiny. A nothing, a nobody, yet in the background I felt the words of Shakespeare echo: *Whose worth's unknown even though his height be taken.*

I felt that somehow I was more than this. Do you ever get this? That invisible yearning, a need to find, to be, or even just touch 'something' that is more than what you are? You cannot quite put your finger on it, but you feel it. It may start as an idea for a better job, a new car, a better relationship, but underneath it all there is a discontent bubbling.

Like Oliver Twist, I just wanted a little bit more.

This was no mere fancy, nor some passing notion of finding greener grass. The deep, dark sigh that came from within my heart was a calling to somewhere I can't describe. It had an abiding, pervasive sense that carried with it a haunted beauty that threatened me with its immediacy. Whether you say it was boredom, or the fickle finger of fate, or a greater destiny, it was a thing that drove me out of my comfortable apartment in Kings Cross, Sydney. Inside ten days that sigh pushed me out.

It was the gestalt of a total tiredness, brought on by a quiet desperation, that in its turn came from the drudgery of inconsequence that my life had turned into.

I was an unimportant wheel, turning a never ending cog, on an endless wheel, that was leading to nowhere. I just wanted a break from it all. That sigh ended a whole chapter of nothingness in my life. One thing is certain, I sigh once more when I sit to write this all down, and still, all these years later, I am not sure why.

The ancients called it the Divine Discontent, an inner drive that sends us into a need to discover something greater than what we are, but at the time it was simply that I had to get out of Sydney and go somewhere quiet where I could write. So I took some time off, and headed out.

Did I mention I was a writer? Seeing as I am here writing this, you really should have already guessed. However, in this instance writing was not the question mark of my life. It was not my search, but more the thing I used to underline a point, in order to understand it better. It filled many hours, and gave my purposeless life some sort of purpose, but on this day it would not suffice. I just needed to do something I felt was of consequence, but nothing seemed to fill the empty hole inside. If I could stop running on this wheel and DO something I would feel better.

I needed to stop, fill up on some nature, and reconnect with the creative person inside.

But of course, this is not the story! It is just what propelled it into being. You might say it is a sadness, but really, it was a need to complete something: To walk the full circle and find the beginning point that I seemed to have lost.

In my life, at that time, I was looking for my origin, my centre. I know this now, though at the time it was a nebulous cloud yet to condense. We all have the journey to something or somewhere before us, and perhaps this tale will give you some impetus to make a decision, to get onto the road to find out, whether the road be less travelled or otherwise.

The Road to Find Out: that journey to the place whereupon all things are made possible. It's like looking for the pot of gold at the end of a rainbow. It's a little like the moon shining on the lake. The reflection on the water is like a road to the moon. It is a dream that seems solid and real, but we know what happens when we try to walk it. And yet, it holds a greater reality, because the road of light points unerringly to the Moon.

It's a feeling that drove me, an important feeling. Anticipation, expectation, the need to discover: All this is really a desire to feed ourselves on something of true worth. It's a contemplation, an ache in the heart, and an understanding of a need to act all at the same time.

Saint Exupery said that it is only with the heart that we see clearly, but what I was looking for was that part of the heart that sees.

As a child I used to spend hours looking into puddles, gazing into nothing in order to find everything. And though you may say, "What has this got to do with sighing? Or this story?" I can assure you it has everything to do with it. Sitting and gazing at a puddle took me on a journey away into secret worlds.

Puddles were my respite from society. Even at Age Three I can remember clearly the anger between my parents, I could feel the distance growing between themselves and the children, a distance increased with every raised voice and ugly look they gave each other. I was the youngest and as the youngest I was the most isolated because, in a sense, I had the most to lose. I had the most to lose because I had never known parents who were happy together. My brothers and sisters had felt a happier time. They had known this happiness was possible, seen it was real. I hadn't, and because of this unknown loss I had no place of respite within. Instead I looked into puddles for hours on end and, in this way, I left my world of trouble and quarrel.

And once there I discovered a wondrous thing: Beauty. A natural and deep intimacy with the moment that is beautiful.

True beauty is found in silence. Between moments it hides, waiting to be discovered, and when you find her she gives you everything. I simply cannot express how deeply I was touched by this intangible thing we call beauty, and it could only be found by removing myself from the troubles, and going within to my private world.

Have you ever had a dream where you are really there? Gazing into puddles was like stepping into a "really here" dream, and exploring worlds that today we might call imagination, but to this sad child, I was there. It was a complete and absolute reality, and far preferable to my external life. It was in the moment of coming back from joy that gave me reason to sigh. So it was in this way I learned how to feel an extraordinary sadness, and as the years passed, I perfected the art of sighing to combat it.

A good sigh is something that is born from long periods of considered thought, and hours of misunderstanding. A sigh is born of a thousand dreams of taking a journey to the heavens, but falling just short. In the dead of night we awake, realise we have missed the dream and are back here on Planet Earth, and indeed: we sigh.

My mother would call me, draw me back from wherever I was travelling as I gazed into my puddle, and I would sigh. But we must get to the tale! This is really why we are here, after all.

In truth, I had almost forgotten this story you hold, and only re-discovered it by accident, buried in an archive of notes that had been stored at my sister's workshop for many years. She was moving, and I had to collect the few boxes that were stored there. Of course, I took a brief look at what was in them, and seeing the title of this book you now hold I remembered this journey that may have otherwise been forgotten.

If I had not had a written journal, I would have otherwise thought this was all a dream.

So what started with a sigh and a need to leave town, to go into the forests to refresh, has ended up as a book.

This brings me to the natural beginning of this tale. At that time in my life I was just so tired with my menial existence, the mediocre job, and my sense of worthlessness. I made myself the promise at that point to take the week off, and that is how I ended up with my camping gear and gold pan up in the mountains. Work had agreed (rather too hurriedly I thought) for me to take leave, and so within 10 days of that first languorous sigh, I was in the woods, alone.

And happy. Free, clear, and happy.

Camping Out

It was a fine autumn day, the perfect day for hiking. Sun was beaming from a cloudless sky and the trees in the forest dappled the ground with shadows. Birdsong lingered in the distance, and the crickets were everywhere. I heard the whisper of the stream, and could smell the coolness of the water as it reached out to call me over.

I was singing away, full of a simple joy, to the tune "Old Man River". Earlier that year I had been invited to sing on stage with a professional opera singer, and had dismally realised how thin my poor voice was in comparison. Yet out here in the wilderness, all on my own with no comparisons to be held, I was free to be myself. So what if it wasn't perfect pitch? What came from me was love, pure and simple.

The contrast of the green that now surrounded me compared to the dull grey tones of O'Connell Street, with all its bankers and accountants was beyond comparison. Mortgages and business is such alien land to me, and I begged to ask: *Why do people willingly enslave themselves to the misery of convention?* Anyone can just up and leave and refresh their soul in nature, so why don't we? When I told co-workers what I was doing for my holidays, they looked at me as if to say, "What, no toilet?"

And when I said I was heading out on my own, it was even worse. "What if you die out there? No one will know!" Someone actually said this! I just looked at them. One: Why would I personally care if I were dead? I mean, I suspect I would be past caring if this were the case. Two: As if that person would care if I were dead? One person asked, "What if there is a nuclear strike? You won't even know it". I scratched my head on that one. Such a curious rational to use to STOP someone leaving the city. After all, if it is going to be destroyed by a nuclear weapon, it's probably best to be elsewhere, yes? But really, this was all because the office folk had this notion that going into the wild was like leaving this universe.

I was so glad to be out of that place. This simple and permanent beauty of rocks and forest fill up the space where my sigh had been. The kindness of this place filled the empty space, and fed that part inside that had long been hungry for spiritual sustenance. I was the fledgling calling out for its mother to feed him, and all around me was my perfect mother. She was feeding me with the sights, smells and sounds of nature. I just wanted to keep walking, soaking up the peace and serenity that oozed from every nook and cranny of the wood, and float in that wonderful place between dreams and reality.

Those offices filled with people who crammed every part of their world with chatter; gossip and secrets were of no consequence to me now: What a suffering. Yet who cared for any of that here? The rattle of never ending tongues crashing against each other in a competition for who was wittier, nastier, cleverer or most talented was already a distant memory. At work all I could think of was getting back to the quiet of my apartment and the comfortable security of my old Remington.

Now, there was nothing but the forest. I was always far more comfortable alone, and in nature, than in the false world of society. Society needs drama, conflict and entanglement to be interesting, yet in the wild you are rich precisely because you have none of it, because you are alone. Alone with life. It's all yours. All of it. And it's everywhere.

To my delight, as I followed the creek I found it led down to a waterfall, one that fell a short distance into an exquisite, small lake. "YES!", I thought to myself, I have found me a big puddle! I realised then how high I had climbed, for the horizon stretched out before me.

Below, on a small plateau that backed up to a semi-circular rock face, there was a cleared area by the lake, fed by a small waterfall. It was an ideal camp site. As the day was already well past 3.00 PM I decided this was definitely my contemplation spot for the next week or so.

Finding my way over the rocks, soon I was tasting the water and listening to the tinkle of the waterfall running down the rock face in front of me. I set about building a ring of stones for the fire, and finding some wood. In just under an hour, with some kindling catching fire, my camp was underway. I quickly put up the tent and prepared the bedroll and then, sitting back with the billy on the boil, I looked about and absorbed the small green valley with the crystal clear lake at its heart. I had come into a special place. Water sang down over the rocks as it fell, the light coloured the sky like a palette, the birds were starting the first strands of their chorus, and the eventide choir would soon begin.

There are no bears or large carnivores to worry about in Australia, but out of habit I always set up a perimeter of twigs, set up to snap if a foot stepped onto them. So, all chores now done I lit my gas lantern to push back the dark, put some beans on the fire, and just laid back to soak up the night song. Complete harmony, that is what I felt. I was back where I belonged, and as the moon rose, a few days off full, her light danced over the ripples of the lake. It was calling me to swim. So, clothes off, I leap into the bite of the cold mountain water.

It was better than any drug. Clear and pure, my mind snapped to a razor sharp awareness, and I felt so alive, so here, so present. Moving back to the fire I feel the whip of the night air bringing me to life. I am now more awake than I had been for months. How do people stay in cities when this is on their doorstep? It still amazes me.

Warm now in my sleeping bag, I drifted away to the song of cicadas, thinking of times past, and family, and friends, and wondering what the hell I wanted to do with my life. At Age 24 I still had absolutely no idea, but just now, right here, it simply didn't matter anymore. Sleep came in her own good time.

Dreams that night took me to odd places, and as I walked through twilight worlds I felt someone was calling my name. I looked about, but there was no one there. I saw a fire on a black lake in a deep cavern, and was entranced, yet at the same time I realised this was something deep within myself. It was an important sign, an omen of sorts, but I could not understand it.

Then a child came up. He was the one who had been calling, and he spoke to me, asking if I was ready to leave yet. I looked behind me, and saw a stairway that led to an open door that showed beyond a beautiful, sunny sky and green field.

For some reason, I could not leave, even though the field beyond was where I preferred to be. I said "No, I can't go yet. I have too much religion in me still." I woke with a shot. It was the middle of the night, the fire was but embers, and the moon had dropped below the horizon. I was deeply shocked, because I had chosen at a very young age that the religion of my mother was not for me.

That was when I first realised that, despite myself, I had absorbed all the guilt, the anger, the fear, and the shame. Despite my best efforts to side-step the burden, like a cucumber too long in the pickle jar, I had been pickled by my upbringing. In the middle of the night, away from the world, I began to see a picture form. And it was not a pretty sight. I saw the ugly, lowly worm within. Most of the decisions and the directions I had taken in my life, I saw how were based on my sense of unworthiness. Guilt and shame were the parents of my belief in personal nothing-ness, and self-loathing was my sibling.

Now you may have already realised this in your own life, and it will come as no surprise. But for myself, out there in the wilderness, it came as a great shock. I had always believed that I was in charge of my life, and though I was a very unimportant person with an insignificant role, I still had hopes and dreams of greater things. To suddenly understand with perfect clarity that your whole life had been driven by the osmosis of a religion into your Soul, one that you had chosen to reject! This was a genuine and lasting shock. I lay there awake, stunned. Like counting sheep to fall asleep, I counted the thousand ways I had made choices based on my sense of guilt and shame.

Finally dawn started to climb into the sky. Somehow my eyes closed and I fell into a dreamless slumber, until the heat of the morning sun woke me up.

It is hard to explain just how this affected me. It was just a dream, yet it was more real than imagination. One on level I felt helpless, like a leaf in the wind, yet on another level I felt as if a real burden I had been secretly carrying was finally revealed.

Somehow the menial job as an underling in an office had been a choice made not by myself, but for me by the burden of unworthiness I carried. Though, by rights, I should have been a Doctor or a Lawyer, I was a nobody. Why? I was hiding. Because I was emotionally stuck in that small, fearful orison I was raised in, I felt I was unable to venture out boldly into life. Yet here I was, out in the wide world.

The really difficult part is facing it. Looking into the darkness, you only see the dark, but now I saw so clearly how guilt and shame had been the driving forces in my life. Yet what could I do about it? These had become a reflex. Some part of me knew that unravelling all of this was going to be a long and difficult process.

These thoughts faded as the day wore on, and walking through the bush rejuvenated my spirits. I had pretty much decided that the office job had to go. Anything was better than the continual, silent disrespect you get shown by people who are but one step higher in the pecking order.

It was in the mid-afternoon that I felt someone else about. Perhaps it was imagination, but I really felt as if someone was there, and making my way back to camp I saw the fire was already set, and smoke was tickling through the trees.

Now in Australia people tend not to carry guns, and violence outside of domestic issues is not a common thing in the bush. But there are hunters, and strange people do exist, so I was cautious about approaching the campsite. I had binoculars with me, so at a distance I climbed a tree, and looked down to discover that a child had apparently gotten lost in the bush. They must have seen the smoke from the fire and found their way to it.

Relieved on one hand, yet disappointed that my private world now had to become a social one, I went to see what the problem was. I called out so as not to surprise the boy, but it was the reverse. As I came up to see the lost child I was shocked to discover I was looking at the same one who had appeared in my dream of last night. He was standing there, hands on hips, looking directly at me.

The Child

He was striking in his confidence. Golden hair, uncombed, with sea green eyes that gazed over a small, straight nose. I could not see his ears, but by the look of him I would not have been surprised if they were pointed, for he seemed all the world like an elf you might find in a Peter Pan comic. He had a very slight, wiry build and wearing forest green and brown clothes that seemed to be made from some sort of leather. I saw no backpack, of anything else someone would carry with them into the bush. All he carried was a sort of defiant curiosity that defies description.

Intrigued I asked, "Can I help you?"

He said nothing, but kept looking at me, quizzically. It was if he had lost something and was trying to find it, and that this something was not me. Finally he spoke, "Isn't it odd how eyes meet before anything else." It was a statement, not a question. "Except our eyes did not quite meet, because when I looked at you, you looked away ever so slightly. Why?"

What do you say to a strange boy, one that you met in a strange dream the night before, who asks you very strange questions like this? I guess I must have glanced away, and right now I felt the need to do this again. It was that odd sense of guilt that had decided where my eyes should look, but I could hardly explain this to a child.

"Is this what you do on your planet?" he continued. "I have seen many people in many places, but never anyone who tries to look as if they are not there with a look."

I blinked. Twice. He remained in place before me, and was clearly not an illusion. Yet perhaps this was a long drawn out sort of dream, and it was still night, and soon I would wake up? He just kept gazing at me as I ran through my thoughts. Some part of my brain picked up the conversation, even as the rest of me wandered in a daze. "This planet? You mean, as in, Earth? Or are we talking metaphorically?" I asked with a laugh, thinking it must be an odd joke.

"I don't think I know 'metaphorically'," he said, simply. "But I speak a lot of languages, so you can try it and I can see if I understand."

Sideways conversations like this were a common practice from my theatre sports days. You had to catch the verbal ball someone threw to you and run with it, ideally to somewhere interesting. Yet for all the world, he seemed so serious, so focused on right NOW. He was maybe very good at theatre, or just very odd, or both.

Truth to tell, in the first moments all I felt was that Guilt and Shame I was made aware of just last night. I felt it again, rising up like bile in my throat. I really had no idea what to say or do, but tried to ape my way through this meeting.

"Where are you from?" I asked.

He looked at me for a long moment, and sighed deeply. Why the sigh? He spoke not a word, but held eyes heavy with thought. "Exactly." he said, as he turned and walked away.

I was left standing helpless. "Pardon me!" I called "I, er, didn't mean to offend you. I just wanted to know if you were lost. Do you need help?" But the child just kept walking, and I was left with this incredible sense of failure. He did not answer, did not even look back, but just vanished into the woods.

What to do? I sat there for long moments wondering. Here was a young child of around eleven years who looked lost in the forest, and I knew I should follow after him and take him back to his parents. Yet I was the one who felt lost! Totally, completely lost in a feeling that I had committed some crime against him.

Cursing myself for my clumsy nature (I was never very good at first meetings) I went about gathering some wood for the fire. Perhaps the child would come back when he was hungry? That was all I could think of. Somehow my short time away from society was no longer a respite. I felt myself falling into a spin of even greater discontent. This confusion I felt had pretty much taken charge of my emotions.

I tried to figure out what I had done wrong, what else I might have said or done, but no matter what alley I followed the blind ending of failure waited there for me. I sighed, and realised that some part of me had instantly liked this child. I was missing his company, or should I say, the company he may have been. What curious omen to see him in a dream, then to meet him face to face.

It had to mean something important, but perhaps now I would never know. Perhaps he would come back, perhaps his parents or scout troop were camped somewhere else, and he wasn't lost.

I gazed into the fire that night, thinking about him. I had even heated a second can of beans and made extra tea, somehow hoping he may have returned, but as the moon rose I found myself alone. Finally I curled up into my sleeping bag, and watched the fire dance over the logs.

Perhaps it was the flash of firelight that got my attention. I must have dozed off, but as I half opened my eyes, there he was, sitting, warming his hands at the fire. It most certainly was the same child, for his flame gold hair was unmistakable. I said nothing, not wanting to frighten him, and just waited and watched.

"Do you think a fire can give as good a reflection as a lake?" he said, presumably to me.

For some reason, I remembered vividly the times I spent gazing into puddles as a child. "It depends on how deeply you look," I said. "I found that puddles hide great secrets if you look long enough, and fires tell me stories as well. It's different from a lake, but everything can tell you a story. Is this what you mean?"

"A secret is an invisible reflection, then?" the child asked of no one in particular. "That could be what I mean."

I surprised myself at this moment. A part of the child that was once me stepped forward, the one that had not been immersed in religion and soaked in fear. "I would look into a puddle when I was very young, and step into other worlds. I would go to other places. The puddle was a doorway. Fire does this for me, as so does the lake. That was my secret. But of course a secret is only a secret if you can't tell anyone about it."

That was it! It just tumbled out, things I have never said to anyone. I don't know where it came from, but then it dawned on me. Because of the religion that ran my family, any talk of these inner journey's I took were always laughed about, ridiculed. "Just imagination child" I would constantly hear. It was just like how my odd notions were laughed about at the office.

"Is it the same secret we see in a fire as we find in a lake?" he asked me, directly. Suddenly those green eyes came alive. "I see many different things, but each of them seems to hold a secret. I want to know what it is."

Was he asking me for the secret to life? "I don't know," I said "But I cooked you some beans, and made you some tea. Are you hungry at all?"

The child leapt up, excited. "Oh YES!" he said. "That's perfect. The secret of your fire is that it lives to feed us, and give us comfort, and tell us stories." I laughed, then got up and stoked the fire, putting the now cold can of beans back on, and the billy, to heat up. It was so odd. Earlier I was despondent, depressed and feeling I had failed again, yet now everything seemed fine. The lad chatted on about things like the night, and the sounds it made, and talked on about all the things that an eleven year old might think of. He hungrily ate the beans, and very happily sipped his tea, and quietly began to fall asleep, yet all the while still talking away. And then he was gone, fast asleep.

I had spare blankets, so I wrapped him up and curled up a pullover for his pillow. Then I just sat by the fire, and watched him sleep. What a perfect, pure child, but why on earth was he out here in the woods alone?

Tomorrow would bring its answers, or at least I supposed this. So happy and content in a way that is difficult to describe, I went to my sleeping bag and slept. Even as I drifted off, I kept wondering if this were all just another odd dream. Would I awake in the morning to find it all gone? It was always a bit of a problem for me, finding out where the line between reality and dreams existed.

A major part of my mother's job was (apparently) to get me to stop day dreaming, and get down to the practical things of life. It was, in my view, a rather hopeless cause. I suspect she might have agreed with me!

"You are supposed to be a professional man," she would say, "but I think you should be a priest."

The Secret

Truth to tell, I lay there that evening wondering about the secret. All my life I had wondered what was the thing behind everything. Terms like "God" or "Spirit" were meaningless to me, because it was something you feel. It was never a thought or a thing you could describe, more a sort of It-ness around you.

Just like nature. Nature has a sort of architectural anarchy, a symphony of opposites if you will, where point and counter point play against each other in a never quite reconciled circles. It is more than carnivores eating lesser species, or trees growing higher than the neighbour to get to the sun. Life itself is imbued with a presence that is shared, and equal, despite the imbalances between types.

Listening to the depth of night I found my ears tuned into a high pitched tone that flowed through the cricket song and seemed part of the universe. I remembered asking my mother about it when I was Five. "What is that sound I hear?" and she said "It's the wind in the wires". Which was fine, because it did sound like that, but there was no wind that day. That was the first time I realised that my Mother didn't know about important things. That was the first time I ever realised I was alone here.

My mind drifted back to the office. It was an abrasive place where no one was doing anything that was natural for themselves, including myself. Everything became stifled by an ever present sense of "should" and the worship of the clock.

I should do this, I shouldn't do that. I would if I could but I won't so I don't. It really wasn't me, but it paid the rent. What I wanted to do was to write, to create music, to talk with interesting people about interesting things, not wear a monkey suit and pretend to be conventional, dull and uninspiring. What the world calls "normal".

So my thoughts rambled on. By the time sleep came I was pretty certain that I was never going back to the office. It's so easy to determine your destiny when you are away from things, yes? Yet so much harder when you are in the thick of it. The rent does have to be paid, after all. Despite these misgivings as to my ability to break away, I slept well

Come the morning, I could have been forgiven for thinking it was all a dream because the child was not to be seen. However, the empty can of beans and the folded up blanket told me that the night had been real. I no longer had that sense of getting it all wrong, and now felt that he would come back when he was hungry. What was it that we were talking about? Oh yes: Finding secrets when looking into a fire.

I had gone out West with my father many times as a child, and the favourite part of the trip was gathering the wood, and watching the animals form in the logs as they burnt. It was uncanny how a dragon would take shape in the flames, and get a fiery 'eye" right where an eye should be, and breath fire out of its mouth just as a real dragon would. It happened again and again, worlds within worlds, shapes within shapes would form and become real for that moment of its existence.

Tibetan Monks do extraordinary sand paintings that take many days, and in the end, they sweep it away to show the transcendental nature of things, and how life itself is imbued with the process of permanent change. This felt like my life, always building towards something, but then the wind would change and the whatever grew would fall back into the dust from which it came.

I wanted to know what was permanent, ever lasting and free. It was what made me into the hopeless dreamer I was. I loved listening to John

Lennon's "Imagine" while on one hand knowing it was impossible, yet on the other saying "Yes, let's Imagine!" Imagine if I were to write a universal declaration. How would it read?

We, the Kaleidoscope of Beings, hereby agree to sing our songs, voice our dreams, and speak our truths without fear or favour. We agree to an anarchy that supports the natural forms. We will respect another's boundaries even as we seek to extend and refine our own. We will do all that we have agreed to do, and will allow others to agree to differ. We hold that our only truths are those which are self-evident, and that each can seek a higher purpose, a better life and a greater sense of self. Amen

I found myself wondering what our little friend would think of these thoughts, and looked about to see where he might have gone. He really did seem so detached from things that it was entirely possible that he forgot to even eat. I heard that Einstein was like that, that he could get so engrossed in his work that he forgot about time and space. Which is quite a paradox, given his work was a proof for its relativity.

The child had an attitude where everything he said, everything he thought, carried with it a weight of consideration. This was something I admired, that he could be so focused on the exact moment of what was in front of him. He seemed to know what was right or wrong for himself, but never did I feel he impinged his beliefs onto mine. I was given complete freedom in his presence.

This was the exact opposite to my upbringing. Fear of hell, a list of invisible "shoulds", expectations on how to act, how to behave, what to do. It was a life where any reward was conditional on approval, and approval was only given to perfection. No wonder I felt that I had failed so often. In my mind I was always fighting these phantom "shoulds".

Where was my instinct? A bird knows what food is right for it, but my diet of imagined rights and wrongs were spoon feeding my heart with poison. I had lost the connection to the natural self by seeking to get external approval for the social self. I needed to stop, I needed to get back to me.

The fire was prepped, the billy was on, and the cobalt blue of the lake beckoned my thoughts. I had my crossword puzzle book out, and I was fiddling in the answers and just feeling the pleasure of the whole day all around me

I wanted to stay here, in this secret spot, yet we all know the pressures of life rarely allow for such luxuries. Soon I would have to return to the humdrum of work, and rent, and social niceties. But not everyone lives like this. I had a batch of friends from school who left home at age 17 and built themselves a lean-to on a mountain on the edge of the city.

They all were pretty happy there, until the police found them and moved them on. That's the problem of living outside of convention. It all lasted but a few months before the heavy hand of society came down, flattening the shack and taking away their freedom of choice. It is no easy thing, finding the balance.

My thoughts meandered like a creek trying to find the ocean. A word for "wandering yet fluent" 7 down, 3 across, 7 letters. Oh or course, meander! I filled it in, laughing at my own stupidity, yet under everything were my thoughts about the child. Would he be OK, and would he return this evening? What would he want to talk about? I found I was missing him. I also found I was starting to get tired of my own thinking. Thoughts can crowd in your head like too many seagulls fighting for a piece of bread. Even the cross word was not enough of a distraction, so I put it down and went with my gold pan to the lake. It was time to stop thinking.

Reason so easily becomes a collection of light and shadow fighting each other. I often look back now at how I out-thought myself at every opportunity. So much time and opportunity was wasted because I thought too much. Rather than trusting life, and just being in this moment, in this flow, I worried it to death.

I was not wasting my hours here, however, for my hands were already fossicking for what I could find by the lake. Even better than the crossword was the joy of discovery of some semi-precious stone. My gold pan yielded no gold, but it had found a strange assortment of other treasures in the sand, particularly at the waterfall that ran into the lake. I also had a veritable harvest of finds, including (surprisingly) quite a bit of amber. You never find amber in water like this. That was always my personal favourite, and today I was fortunate enough to pick up some clear stones, as well as a few odd semi-precious crystals.

I put them onto a large rock I had set near the fire, because I wanted to see how they glowed in the firelight. Indeed, I had gathered a number of rocks, making a sort of table-come-altar for my odds and ends. In the fading light I was looking through the few clear crystals I had found, seeing what patterns formed while I whittled away at finishing the cross word puzzle from that morning.

That was when I heard his voice. "What are you doing with your notepad?" I looked up and there he was.

My heart leapt with joy! I was very glad he was back. "Hello little friend," I said. His peach complexion had not suffered from the rigours of the bush, so I suppose he must have stayed in the forest through the day. "I am working on a crossword puzzle." I showed him the puzzle.

"I used to hear cross words from my Rose, but I do not think she ever really meant it." He sighed, obviously away in some memory where I could not go.

"No, not cross as in angry," I said. "Cross as in one word crosses the other and they all link up. You see, here 'Meander' crosses 'sandwich' on the 'n' … That's a crossed word. See?" I show him.

He looked puzzled, so I explained how you are given a clue, and the code for where the word that answers the clue must go. I gather he had never seen a crossword before, because he found it fascinating, and funny, as we sat and worked out some of the answers together.

"I see. This is a little like life. You are given a hint, and the answer for this moment connects with another moment, and that's how you know you are on the right track." Right at that moment a glint of fire must have caught the amber, because he stopped completely, and in wonder just gazed at it.

"Why have you got all those rocks about you?" he asked.

"They are not just rocks, little one. They are special rocks. Have you ever seen amber or crystals?"

I handed some over for him to look at. "You never know what secrets you will find in something that looks ordinary," I said, and gave him a small jeweller's glass and showed him how to use it. "Look and see if you find anything beautiful."

He was absolutely entranced by this small offering, and looked, and stared for ages at the various bits and pieces I had handed him. He made the odd sound, a sort of excited murmur, but he said nothing in particular. He reminded me of myself at a young age, always completely fascinated by the slightest bit of science, and totally happy when my thoughts were occupied in some adventure.

It gave me the opportunity to really study him, this boy whose name I did not know. There was nothing of him, really. He was very slight, yet at the same time I had the impression that he was tough, despite the pale, soft English skin, and hands that had clearly not worked fields. His fingernails were well manicured, so he could not have been out here long, but he was in the same clothes as yesterday. I wondered what on earth he had been doing, how he got here, and where his parents were. But I said nothing because I did not want to break the spell.

Those sea-green eyes had a piercing quality and a dance of bright awareness in them. Again and again he went back to a particular crystal, and wanted to see more of it. "This one seems special, yet it does not come alight like the others. What is it?" he asked me.

I took a look; it appeared to be a piece of common Rhodonite. "Some of these crystals have to be cut to reveal their secret," I said. "You can never be sure until you open it up, and see what is really inside. Look, I will take this piece of common Amber and put a polishing cloth to it. Watch what happens."

I took the dull amber, and using some polishing compound cut the roughness from the surface and put the translucent stone up near the fire, inviting the child to have a look. He did so, and his jaw dropped. "It is SO beautiful" he said, so I gave him the polishing cloth and suggested that he might want to see what he could find in some of the other bits of Amber I had found. He took to it eagerly, and as the sun fell, he sat there polishing away while I prepared some boiled eggs, with toast and tea for our evening meal.

My thoughts drifted back to when the doors had shut on my childhood. There was no definite day or event it happened, but somewhere along the line my natural self was called childish, and I wanted to be grown up. That's when the shoulds took hold, that is the zone where we give up the natural state, and start taking on the social persona. Only I was never very good at it.

It seemed such cruelty, looking back, that we adults could inflict their burdens and sufferings onto our children with nary a thought to their freedom. My own son had been taken away by a jealous mother. She knew he preferred myself to her, so she took him at age three, and told me she had found God, and that God had said I was not to see him. I still grieved, but I also knew that fighting to get him back would mean only pain for him. She was a vindictive creature who would make sure she damaged him rather than see him happy with me.

Perhaps this was why my heart had gone out so completely to this one? I can't really say, but what I know is that I felt an intense joy watching him polish the amber and look at the stones.

"It's so beautiful, yet moments ago it was dull and lifeless. How can this happen? How can we discover beauty when it is hidden?" he asked.

Something about the way he asked questions went straight to the heart. Man oh man, I thought to myself. That's the big question. I answered, "That was no ordinary rock I gave you, young Sir. It is a piece of amber, and amber, when polished and loved and treated well, begins to find itself and learns to shine. You would think the sun itself has been trapped in there, wouldn't you?" the child nodded agreement, "Well this is in part because it took the sun to make it. Would you like to know more?"

He nodded, "Yes please."

Well, you know the trees? Of course you do, well the sap from these trees is a living thing, it is like the trees blood and it is made because the sun draws the life up from the ground, and the sap brings the water and food that allows the tree to grow. Yet if we capture this tree sap, and if we put it under great pressure for a long period of time, it turns to this stone we call Amber. It's beautiful, despite how common and ordinary it started, because of what it has gone through."

A great tear rolled down his face, and it truly surprised me. What sadness could there be in this? Yet the tear held with it an immeasurable pain and solitude. "I was once a Prince," he said quietly, in a manner that is impossible to describe other than to say it made me feel like shedding a tear as well. "But my Rose died and my little planet was left with no heart, no ideal to make life worthwhile. That's why I left, and this is why I wander all over the universe."

I waited, but he spoke no more. The silence became a heaviness, so I proceeded with my demonstration. "Now here we see a rock that you would imagine was nothing but a plain, dull stone, yes?" he nodded, still wrapped up in sadness. "Well let's see if we can change this," and I took out my little chisel, and gave the rock a sharp tap in the right place, showing the heart of the stone.

"OH!" he cried, eyes opening like balloons being blown up, "but this is marvellous and wonderful. Again you take something ordinary and turn it into beauty. How do you do this?"

"It isn't me that does this, lad. I just show you what is hidden, and I can show you because I have learned what stones hide secrets, and which ones are merely stones. The beauty is already there, it just takes the right tap in the right place to reveal it. The hard part is learning which rocks have potential, and which don't. And not all that look as if they may be

OK work out. Some rocks are just rocks, yet others are truly special. Like this one."

The boy stood up, and despite all his youth he did indeed look like a Prince. The sadness of moments ago had blown away like a leaf in the autumn winds. He looked right at me, and said with utter certainty. "Yes, you are right. We spend so many hours thinking and believing we have discovered something beautiful, but unless it opens up to us, we can never truly know.

"And until WE show our beauty, until WE open up and reveal what we are inside, we can never really know if we are special or just another rock in a field of stone that is dreaming it is something bigger and better than it truly is. Thank you, you have helped me clear up a very great mystery and taken a burden from my heart."

What could I say? I hardly considered my words to be that wise, yet his obvious sincerity left me feeling somewhat shy. Finding no words to say, I let the silence speak. After all, a man only appears foolish when he tries to continue a conversation past it's natural ending.

I handed him his eggs, toast and tea, and we sat listening to the night, watching the moon rise, and feeling the swift bite of the night air upon our backs. I gave him a blanket, roughed up a sort of pillow with clothes in a pullover and in due course I curled up in my sleeping bag to watch the dragons and crocodiles take form in the fire once more.

He spoke just one more time that evening. "You can see light come from what was once darkness in your stones, yet both the light and the darkness must have been there all along, and they must have been in harmony because the stone was content to lie where it was. Is one any better than the other?"

I had no idea. "I can't say, but I can say that I like gemstones, and I love finding the ones that are special. It gives me joy and I don't think the gems mind being discovered. I certainly like finding special things inside me, so maybe stones feel the same way."

"Maybe it is more a case of understanding our destiny, and allowing ourselves to shine, that is the secret?" the child said as he trailed off into worlds of his own.

My eyes must have shut, because I remember nothing else other than listening to the cicadas as they drowned out everything else. Oddly, I had one thought, about how difficult it must have been for the apostles to remain awake at the Garden of Gethsemane. When you are surrounded by beauty, your hard mental will to follow the rigid path of disciple weakens, and then it is so easy to shut the eyes and dream.

Conversely: When our duty overtakes an appreciation of the moment, it becomes tarnished. It is like covering up the inner light, and stopping yourself from shining.

Can a Lake be Wise?

That morning I woke to see the blanket once more folded, but this time the child was nearby. He was down at the lake, gazing out over it into nowhere. He seemed transfixed by some invisible, distant dream.

I moved quietly out of my sleeping arrangements, so as to not disturb him, and just felt the sun. It was perhaps a half hour past dawn and I had been happily dreaming in the warmth of it until the rays became a heat. I cannot remember a time I had been more content, and seeing my little friend was still here brought a real smile to my heart. Why could the rest of my life not echo this moment?

I got my toothbrush and towel, and went down for my morning wash. He didn't give any indication he was aware I had woken, standing there like a tattoo on the landscape. Even as I went down near him, he remained fixed on his inner horizon. Having nothing in particular to say, I said nothing and waited for him to speak.

It was perhaps only a few minutes, but it seemed like a very long time before he spoke. "Do you think a lake can be wise? He asked. A good question: If I could get so much from a puddle when I was a child, would a lake offer more? Yet surely we can only see wisdom already within us.

"Perhaps we see ourselves in all things, yet the peace of the lake, its stillness, allows us an undisturbed view?" I offered. Yet even as I said it, I was wondering how many thousands of puddles and rain drops had gone into the making of this place. Water had been sucked up from distant oceans, tossed up into clouds, and sent down as rain on the mountains to finally rest here, in the lake.

"The fire offers different stories to water, but they both speak stories to my heart," he said. "These stories I hear are not mine. No one owns then, and yet DO I own them. Like drops that make this lake, now they have become part of the whole story of my life."

He was clearly so involved in his own thoughts that all I was hearing was an echo. I remained silent to let him continue. "When I walk along the limb of a tree, I own the journey, and within me the tree now lives forever. It all depends how deeply you see," he murmured to no one. It struck me that he wanted to say more, but there were no more words.

"How deeply we see?" I prompted. "Do you mean into ourselves, into what is before us, or into the moment?"

He looked right up into my eyes, and I felt a sort of electric shock. It surprised me, because he seemed so helpless, yet here I met a tiger, hungry for his truth. "Wisdom is not what it seems. All the wisdom in the universe will not save a flower from dying. Wisdom is just the understanding we used up in practice, hoping to get it right." He trailed off, going back to his distant place, saying as he left, "I think I understand now what the gardener told me."

Then he stopped completely. He was gone, away, only his body stood before me. It seemed as if the child had left for a distant world. "A gardener?" I asked, hoping to draw him back. "What gardener?"

Something stirred in him. "Oh, the man I met shortly after the salesman had come to sell me the Jewel." he said rather absent-mindedly, not really hearing my interest.

"The salesman?" I asked.

"Yes, a very strange fellow, but he did teach me something."

"Would you like to tell me about your salesman?" I asked, "Because I would like to listen, if you wished to talk." It was like fishing, trying to catch this elusive conversation, yet who was fishing and who had taken the hook? I simply wanted to know everything I could about this remarkable young man. Perhaps it was that he had a certainty I would have liked for myself? Yet, more than the curiosity I felt, in his tales there was something important.

"I was on my planet, very upset because my Rose had died. You see, I left her in order to understand love but when I finally returned I understood only that I was a fool. Love just IS and cannot be understood, but it was too late, she had already passed away. Of course, she was a flower, and so must fade. But she was MY flower, and I had left her."

"To be fair, I cannot say for certain that she is dead. All I know is that there was no rose when I returned. Perhaps someone came by and snipped her, and took her to their home. Yet when you love someone, and they are not there, it is like death."

"But surely," I suggested "if someone left, they could write a letter, or send a message?"

"Flowers are very poor letter writers." The child corrected. "And even if she were alive, and chose not to speak to me, then all my world knows is loss. For me she is dead. Not that I love her any less for this, of course. In truth, I love her more because now I cherish the moments we had. I can remember the sweet and forget the sad. And there was sad, because when I was with her, I suffered."

"You loved a flower even though it caused you to suffer?" I asked.

"Oh it was a beautiful suffering. Pain is not at all a bad thing if it causes you to find happiness," then he sighed. "Yet all the learning in the world could not fill the emptiness I was feeling when I came back to find her gone. That was when the Salesman arrived."

The Salesman

Hello there!" said the salesman with gusto. "Ain't this just the most beautiful day you have ever seen? I must say, I am so pleased to meet such a fine soul as yourself on this fine day!"

"To be perfectly honest" said the child as he related to me this story, "I felt very uncomfortable at first. The Salesman seemed to smile far too much to be real, and I felt he was a little untrustworthy. However, to be courteous I replied in kind, saying that it was indeed a fine day. I really had nothing more to say, so we just looked at each other for a few minutes."

The salesman took conversational matters into his own hands. "Why this is a fine planet as well. I think you could get a great trade on this one, a really good deal if you are looking to upgrade, you know, more land, better ferns. There is a perfect place over in Alpha Prime, a new planet. One that has not even been walked on yet. It's a great neighbourhood, no slums AND it's on the prestigious left bank of the Clown Nebula. You'll love it!"

"Why would I want a new planet? I am perfectly happy with this one, thank you very much." Looking back to me and breaking from the telling of his story, he whispered "I really thought he would have just gone away at that point, but he seemed very insistent on carrying on."

The salesman was unfazed. "Tell you what, Kid. I can see why you don't want to leave. It's a good planet, you are used to it, it's comfortable BUT once I show you some options you might just start to think maybe, you might think maybe not. And if it is maybe, you just will not believe the deal I can do for you. I am talking HIGH trade in, LOW ingoing, really cheap interest and a better exchange price than you will get anywhere in the universe.

"Spend your money with me kid, and you will never regret it. I make 100% sure that my customers not only get the best deal, they get better than the best deal. I am talking quality, I am talking refinement, I am talking anything you can imagine and we can find it for you."

The child watched as the salesman pulled out some money, a thing that was quite unfamiliar to him, saying "You got the money, kiddo, and we get you the world. Literally, I mean ANY world, cause they are ALL for sale."

"Well, I don't have any money, nor do I need it.

"Absolutely correct young fella! You DON'T need cash. We can organise the finance, and there you go. That spankingly beautifully brand new planet is yours. Just think of the new sunsets, the better horizon, the new visitors you will get in your better, upgraded place of residence."

"No, what I mean is that I don't need money because I am happy where I am. I don't want to trade my planet, and I really don't want to leave it for another one. We like each other, my planet and I, and I am happy for it to stay this way."

The child broke once more from the tale "I found it very difficult to speak because this fellow seemed to be almost shouting the whole time, but then I realised that I had been asking the universe to send me someone to answer my question about what to do. With my rose gone I felt quite lost, you see. Perhaps this man had something I needed, so I decided to ask him directly."

"I do have something missing though. I did have a rose, but she died."

"Well gee whiz kid. Roses do that sometimes. Just when you get to like them, they are yesterdays memory, but no problem, no problem at all. It's your lucky day because I have one right here." and with this the Salesman pulls out a fine tudor rose.

The child looked up again from his telling of the story. He had that distance back in his eyes, as if he remembered something that actually happened. At the time, I thought it was a wonderful make-believe, but I started to see he really did believe in it. I could tell that, for him, it was a complete reality. So I kept listening ...

"It was a very beautiful rose. 'Hello.' I said to it, 'What's your name?' but it didn't answer me. It just stayed there, silently. It may have looked beautiful, but it was cold."

"It doesn't talk?" he asked of the salesman.

"Roses can be like that sometimes, hey? Looks great, smells fabulous, would be brilliant on the mantelpiece, but it just doesn't speak to you. I know exactly where you are coming from kid! But the sad thing is I don't got no talking roses. Let's face it, you are lucky I could find this one. Roses are pretty darn thin on the ground around here you know. But you are right, it doesn't talk, so we can look at it for a discount, yes? I mean to say, let's get the price to do the talking for us, OK?"

"No thank you" said the child, "It's a lovely rose, but it's not my rose" and with this he moved away from the salesman.

"Kid, hey kid. Don't walk away. Tell you what, I have just the thing to cheer you up, something that will really impress you. Take a look at this!"

In his hands was the most beautiful thing the child had ever seen. It glittered and sparkled as if the sunlight seemed to flow through it with a life of its own. It looked as if it held the secrets of a thousand years. "What is it?" he asked.

"Yes indeed. What is it? That's the question to ask young man, and I can see how astute you are in recognising it's inherent loveliness. Girls go ape over these things, and if you want to impress, boy you just can't do better than this. This is a full three carats of diamond perfection, and the story that goes with this stone will blow your mind. Dug from a dry well on Beaumont 3 by a dog that fell in when snuffing for truffles. And it is yours for the measly price of, say, a 30 year lease on this little planet of yours. Or, if you want to stay here, I can arrange easy repayments to suit. Do we have a deal?"

I have to say, I started to laugh, and so did he. The child looked up at me from where he was acting out the story, puffing himself up very big to play the part of the Salesman, then getting small for himself, "I looked at that stone for a long time. It was indeed very beautiful, but the more I looked the more it felt to me that the beauty was not of the heart. I began to realise that the special something I was missing was kindness, not beauty.

"What I was looking for was something in MY heart, something alive and though this stone appeared alive, and held great fascination, it had no soul. I knew that one day the surprise I felt gazing into it would wear off and I would be left holding the echo of a dream. I had to find something that would not fade, or run away, or die."

"No thank you," I said to the Salesman. "This is not the special thing I need, and I do not think that the secret wish I hold in my heart is for something that can be bought or sold."

"Kid, you sure are a tough customer. Someone who wants something that can't be bought or sold is looking for a hard road. Believe me, it is a lot easier to settle for something that gives you the lift you need right now. If it wears off, you can always sell it, and buy something else.

"That's how it all works, kid! Now if you want to fight against the tide then all power to you, but when you change your mind, and people always do change their minds, which is why I stay in business, then you get back to me, OK? The salesman handed the child a card with the phone number "800 Buy the World" on it and he left, obviously to some other planet where he could sell his goods.

The child looked at me earnestly. "I was very tempted you know. It was a very beautiful stone, this diamond, and it did have a lovely story to go with it. But in my heart I knew it was an empty creation, and that what I needed was an intangible, invisible something and I had to trust that I would know it when I came across it. It was this meeting that convinced me I had to search for what I needed, and this is why I was called to leave my planet, and travel to distant places.

"And this is what brought you here?" I asked, gently trying to get some background on the boy.

He looked at me quizzically for a moment, as if trying to figure out how this question fitted in with what he was saying. "Well, no. My journey took me to a very different place to here, though I must suppose that 'here' is indeed part of my journey. What happened is that when the Salesman left I felt this terrible sadness, and it caused a great tear to fall from my eye, which left a small puddle in the ground, which created a light beam to break up into a small rainbow as it shone through it.

"As I gazed into the rainbow, I fell in and it took me up and away from my home, to special worlds where I learned so much more about life and living."

"Did you want to tell me about your travels?" I ventured.

I got that deep piercing look again, only this time I did not look away. I wasn't afraid anymore of what he might see, I suppose. It is odd how, as the heart opens, we allow ourselves to be more honest and more free. "Yes," he said "I would like to tell you. It's important to share things, because our stories are like seeds that when given to another can help them to grow their own garden of truth."

So, despite all this preamble, this is where our tale truly begins. It is a tale that I found to contain a deep, yet simple wisdom. I will simply relate it as best I can recall and leave it to yourself to determine the value of the content.

The Gardener

He looked out over the hills that surrounded the Lake and gave out another sigh. I am not sure if it was regret, weariness or simply the difficulty of trying to find words. I suspect the latter, as it would seem he was not used to long conversations with anyone other than himself.

"I had fallen into the rainbow, and they are capricious things. You never know where you will end up, and you have no clue as to how to get back to where you were. On this day, though, I fell into a really lovely Garden."

"A Garden?" I asked "Whose garden?"

He looked at me strangely and said "Why, the gardener's, of course." He paused, I presume to make sure the obvious had entered my brain, then continued. "There I was, dropped by that rainbow right into a flower bed. The fragrance was lovely, but I was sure that the person who looked after this garden would not like someone sitting on his rhododendrons, so I got up as quickly as I could.

"Yet it was difficult, not because I was hurt, but because the fragrance from all the flowers made you very lazy. All I wanted to do was sit there, and dream. In fact, it seemed to me that the beautiful scent came from everything there, not just the flowers. The whole place was soaked in this marvellous smell. I was completely at peace, and yet strangely, completely out of sorts.

"I can't explain it. The pain of loneliness has vanished, but nothing had really come to replace it. It was then that I first saw the gardener. I watched as he tended each plant, every single one got his full attention and he spoke to them all as if they were old friends enjoying the day. For some reason, I became completely fascinated just seeing how he treated every single flower, and part of me remembered how I had to fuss and look after my rose. That seemed a very great effort, yet for this man it was no trouble at all.

"Then I saw him stop by a very sick flower, and his whole being seemed to change. He spoke softly, and whispered kind words to it, and said that he hoped she would get better soon. And for some reason, I started to cry. I don't know why, but as a tear welled up in my eye, the Gardener looked right at me. Until that moment I was sure he didn't even realise I was there, but now I stood transfixed by his gaze. That was when I asked him about my Rose"

"Why do flowers die?"

The Gardener stopped his work, and looked more closely at the odd new addition to his garden. His sharp eyes seem old, yet young at the same time. There was a twinkle in them. His bald head indicated he was some sort of monk. Maybe this was a Monk Garden?

"Why does beauty fade? All things have their time, child. You wonder why life just takes its own direction, regardless of whether we agree with it, or whether it makes us feel sad, or otherwise? Do you really wonder why Life will just do what it will do?" The Gardener asked with a raised eyebrow.

Without any effort the Gardener had pierced to the heart of the matter. I said nothing and just watched the face of the child, and as he retold his tale his amazement came through. "How could he have known so clearly what my problem was?" he said to me, "I had thought it was loneliness, but in truth my real sadness came from why Life acted in a way that seemed so unkind."

"Yes." I said to the Gardener. "I have thought about this very thing a great deal. Why does something so beautiful have to die?"

He looked up at me, coming back from that far distant world he was in. "The Gardener said nothing for some time, and just continued gazing into my eyes. I felt like one of his flowers, being cared for, looked after. Finally he spoke, to say:"

"Yes indeed little friend. Yes indeed. All things must fade until they discover the Power of Lasting, which is no power at all, but a surrender to the flow of life. It is a trust that all is in the right place and at the right time. Despite how our dreams fail, and how things seem to go wrong. we are all on the journey to discover what really lasts."

The Gardener paused, then continued. "Your real question is: *How do we best survive?* Well, to be alive means that life is flowing through us, yes? So to survive all we need do is allow our life to flow. The real question is: What stops the flow? It is our fear and hatreds that block life, and it is our love that releases it. So we either move forward with love, or retreat from life with fear.

"This is the true Law of the Worlds. We all have our fears and sad times but the choice of what we do with these is what makes our life. It is not the events we meet, but the choices we make. You may not believe it, but even a Flower makes this choice. She may not have legs, but she has a heart, and when this moves on in any friendship, the part that was cherished fades, and it appears that your flower dies.

"But where do we go? The events of our life and our feelings and our thoughts are like building blocks. We can use these to build a wall to defend ourselves against life, or we can use them as a bridge to meet it. So we either fall within, or we expand and grow into our next adventure. That's our real choice, and everyone has this freedom.

"You see, you suffered a loss, and you feel pain. But it's not what happens that counts, it's what we choose to do with it. When we choose to build a bridge to something greater every day, then we discover that within us a bridge to the highest and purest part of ourselves. It's just that simple.

"The promise of tomorrow is found in the choices we make right now." The Gardener stopped, looked to the sky as if expecting rain, and gathered his thoughts.

"It is really about gathering ourselves. People rarely spend the time to embrace their moments, and so they lose them. Rather than stopping to cherish the small things, most people just want something big. Yet every big thing comes from many small things that work together. Cherish the moment, and we grow to cherish our life.

"And if we wish to cherish our life, we must sustain our love for life. This is the secret. This helps our imagination not to get lost, dreaming about the promise to come. This is what keeps us with the reality that is Now. Why? Because when we really appreciate a person or a thing for what they are, right now, this it is like watering a flower. Just stand back and watch it grow.

"That's why I love being a gardener. I watch things grow, yet it is true, I also watch things pass on. My choice is to stay with the growth, and cherish my garden even as I allow nature to take its course. What else can we do?

Then the Gardener took the dying flower into his hand, "We are all dying, we are all falling, we are all becoming less until we learn to love. Surely each moment will pass, but when we flow with life, so too will our appreciation, and our love flow to the next moment. Appreciation and Love. This simple gratitude sets us free.

"I love this flower, but do I try to stop things by saying 'Don't leave!' or do I trust that life will bring us everything we need?

"By letting go, you set yourself free. This is the simple law. The river flows eternal, but it is always passing. Try to dam the river, and the pressure builds up, the sadness grows, and the tears we shed break the banks. And this, too, is good, because at last you are letting it flow.

"This endless change, this continual movement of life: It is a thing to be embraced not feared. All the world is richer for this flower, so why pine when its time has come? It will last in my heart for as long as my heart shall last.

"When we fill the heart with small but important riches like this, each moment becomes something more. We become deeper so that more life can flow into the cup of our being. So I ask you: Why would anyone choose the poverty of lost and lonely dreams when we have such riches surrounding us?"

The child spoke up, at last, to the Gardener, "But if I am unhappy, surely I must search for that which will make me happy?"

"If we are unhappy, we must search for better choices, not solutions." answered the Gardener, quite simply and clearly. "What do you imagine your heart hears when you are telling it you are looking for happiness? It hears that you are not happy, and it grows sad for you. Just choose a new path, and walk it. The decision for a new direction is an affirmation of life, the search for happiness is the loss of it.

"That was when the light of understanding got me," the child pulled back from his tale, and grew quite serious. He looked at me, saying, "You see, I had loved my rose for the promise of beauty she offered. I cared for what she was, but I had hoped for something greater to come.

But did I ever ask my Rose what she wanted? I forgot that she is the one who chooses her future, not I."

ooo000ooo

I thought about these words. We have all done it, gone head over heels with a crush on someone but they choose to leave for whatever the reason and we, in turn, are crushed. We imagine so much promise for us, but do they?

All the soap operas in the universe revolve around the lost promise of romantic dreams. We are all trying to fill up holes with space, cursing life for the pain it gives us, or perhaps we are worshipping someone with unrequited hope.

Just choose a new direction? Is it really that simple? As I thought about it, it occurred to me that I chose to leave the office to find peace in nature. I guess in part it was a search for happiness, but it was really a choice to be free. And look where that decision has led me!

Ooo000ooo

"The Gardener has whispered to me, not with words, but heart to heart. He seemed to say that I need not despair. My problem was that while I had found a moment, I had not found forever in the moment. The beauty I was seeking was deeper than I had looked. That was all that the problem was, but that somehow to look deeper meant I also had to look further. I was unsure about this, so I followed him around for most of that day. Finally I asked him, 'Do you know why I am here?' "

He looks at me earnestly. "I wanted to know why I had fallen into a rainbow and ending up in his garden."

The Gardener laughed. "You are here because you are looking for the Pot of Gold at the end of the rainbow, and this is where your rainbow brought you. As to WHY you are looking for a Pot of Gold, well I don't trouble myself with those sort of questions any more. But you can tell me if you wish."

"All I know is that a beautiful flower, a Rose, left me, and a Salesman tried to sell me a jewel. It was beautiful, and certainly would have been less argumentative than my Rose, but it had no heart, and it didn't speak to me. On one hand I had a Jewel that showed me all its beauty, but had no promise of anything more than this, and yet on the other I had a Rose that showed me nothing, but was full of promise.

"Should I have contented myself with the pretty jewel, and just accepted that what it had to give was all it had? Or should I continue to look for the promise of my Rose?"

The Gardener laughed a huge laugh, one that shook his whole being. "Oh child, you have already answered your question. You are here, far away from your planet, and already on your journey."

"But, am I pursuing a dream? Will I find what I am looking for?"

The sun was setting, the cool of the evening breeze was moving across the fields, and the flowers were all closing their eyes and falling asleep. The Gardener stood for some time before answering, and finally he spoke: "It is not the seeking that finds, it is not the finding that fulfils, it is not the answer that satisfies. Only your connection to life will show you what you need to know. Life speaks in a single, clear voice. And it is only the person certain in all they do that hears clearly the single voice.

"You are looking for the One, but your thoughts are many. You seek the heights of understanding, yet you dig for answers. You look everywhere, but you don't yet even know what is looking. Stop and see what is here. Truth is always a fruit plucked from a tree you find in your own backyard. You will know it when you taste it."

Finally the child said what was truly on his mind. "You have many flowers, many souls to love you and to be loved by you, but I had only my rose, and she is gone."

The Gardener waved his hand over his garden. "Do you imagine I came here with this garden already formed? No, I too had a flower that I loved, and she passed away. But she gave me seeds, child. She gave me the seeds I needed, and in planting these more flowers grew. As more flowers grew, the bees came. As the bees spread their pollen, and as birds flew to nest here, other flowers were brought in by nature, and slowly my garden took shape.

"So the real question is: What seeds were left you by your Rose?"

I must have looked puzzled, because the Gardener bent down, and looked directly into my eyes. He grew very serious, as if this was something that I needed to remember. "Every seed is a small thing, yet it grows to something much more. Your loneliness is a seed that brought you here, and started your journey, but what will grow if it?

"This garden exists because many small seeds were tended to. All things of consequence in our life are really the gathering of many small things of no apparent importance, yet this only makes the small things VERY important.

"All big things are made from many small things. This is what every big thing should always remember, and what every small thing should never forget."

"To be perfectly honest," the child said looking up at me. "I barely heard what he was saying because I was quite upset. I had thought my love for my flower to be special and rare, but he seemed to be saying my rose was nothing. All that mattered were the seeds. But though seeds might grow a rose, it would not be MY rose.

"I was also getting so very tired and sleepy, but I wanted to know more. I called out in the fading light: 'Maybe I should just accept the Jewel the Salesman offered!' Even though it might not be able to talk to me at least it would last. At least I could have faith that it would be there when I got back. At least it would not cause me the pain of loss!' "

The perfume of the flowers overpowered me. As I fell back into some deep well of irresistible sleep, I heard the parting words from the Gardener speaking to my heart. "Ah, but you have been touched by a greater love young one. Despite yourself, one day you would remember this, and then the jewel you held would become a reminder that you were holding something less than your greatest love, and this would tarnish it. Once you have been bitten by true love, you can never be happy with something less.

"Perhaps it is time for you to go on a journey to a different place and time, one where a Jewel was very important."

The boy stopped his tale at this point, I was not sure why. He just disappeared into his thoughts. However it was midmorning by now, and time for tea and an overdue breakfast. We went from the lake and came back to our little camp in silence. I prepared our food, and then he spoke once more, this time he started telling me of the strange dream he had that night when he stayed in the place of the Gardener. The dream about the Jewel of Truth.

The Jewel of Truth

It was a Garden of Dreams, the legendary place of Evermore found only in the laughter of children and caught only in the special moment where all doubt and fear subside, and leave an impenetrable stillness within the heart.

It was here in God's own garden that the two children of Light, Ilniah and Iesa. They played and danced with the singing music of creation. This mysterious power flowed through all things, and sang sweet melodies as it ran over the flowers and trees. There was no before or after, no here or there, just an ever-present song of Now.

Freedom flowed like nectar from a cup, carrying with it a joy that reached to the far ends of existence. Just as a ripple flows out from a stone into the pond, every moment of laughter and every joy you felt sent waves of greater happiness through the forest.

Those who speak of truth are rarely those who know it. But any who have travelled to this Eternal Garden find only depth and serenity as they swim in this unfathomable river. In this moment exists all of life. Every moment is complete, and as the next moment arrives, it joins with the last, like a drop joins a river. Deeper and deeper it flows, until its song becomes the heart song of all beings.

Night never falls in this wondrous place, and no shadows exist to echo a loss of light. In this world beyond time and beyond space, all are a light unto themselves, a true spark, a part of the Divine.

Yet nothing in this garden carried the light and beauty more purely than the ancient Jewel of Truth. This gift was divinity itself, and any who were lucky enough to find it would marvel at the incredible sight. You could feel the wondrous texture that the very air about it pulsed with. Your heart would be fit to burst with the swelling of joy you felt in such a place. Yet you could never touch it.

Ilniah and Iesa used to play near the Jewel often, and would bask for long moments in its radiance. But never did it come close enough to touch. If you reached for it, it would shimmer and seem to bend in and away from your grasp.

Finally Iesa asked why this were so. She was deeply curious, and started to focus on the jewel, ignoring Ilniah until he asked her what she was doing. "Ilniah, tell me … Why does this beautiful Jewel always stay at a distance? Why does it never come close?"

Ilniah was pure of heart and clear of thought but this question caught him unawares. "I know not, Iesa. It is what it is. Perhaps the Jewel simply chooses to be so, and there are no answers but this."

Iesa kept up her vigilance. "But why does it linger giving only the rays of its Love, not it of itself? Are we unworthy of it?

Ilniah had no way to respond, nor sought to give any except to take his playmate once more to the joy and pleasure of their games. He rejoiced in seeing her smile and adored the spirit that flowed through her. Iesa, forgetting her questions, fell back into play and once more whimsy and frolic filled the air about them.

Again their moments passed uninterrupted, or so it seemed. But at quiet times, just before sleep or when looking out over the perfect world that was their garden, Iesa would feel the bite of her questions once more. Doubt had taken seed in the invisible recesses of the heart, and more and more her thoughts turned from play to the question about the jewel. Slowly she was drawn into introspection thought, until it seemed to Ilniah that Iesa had left him for her own private world. More and more he was left to wander the Eternal Garden alone.

There was no pain in this parting, because Ilniah had not yet learned what pain might be, yet he felt sad in ways he could not express. Iesa had moved closer to the Jewel, and now spent most of her waking time in its presence, just gazing into it, occasionally trying to touch it. But always it danced just out of her grasp.

As moments passed they seemed to slow down for Ilniah. He felt the lack of a playmate not as a hindrance, but as a deepening curiosity. And just as Iesa grew preoccupied with the jewel, Ilniah came to wonder all his waking moments about why she was so preoccupied, ignoring him. He, too, came to wonder about the purpose of the Jewel, and wanted to know why it was here.

The nights seemed to grow colder, the wind seemed to blow less sweetly, and less and less joy and laughter could be heard echoing through the woods. Precious moments stood alone, waiting for the next moment when they would be welcomed into the heart, but the door was shut to them.

Ilniah would think of the past, yet now it seemed as a dream. It was there, yet it was elsewhere, and for the first time he started becoming acutely aware that he was alone. As more moments languished, Ilniah could see Iesa in the distance, entranced in the riddle of the Jewel. Finally discontent began to arise in his heart. He wanted to know why she was so attracted to this Jewel.

"Iesa" he called out "why do you choose not to play? Why do you spend all you moments gazing at this gem while the world about us waits unattended?" She did not even answer, but continued to stare into the

Jewel, occasionally reaching out and watching it move away from her outstretched hand.

For Ilniah each moment now seemed to stretch into an eternity of nothing. His thoughts became as a slow, arduous river struggling to find its way to the ocean. The pure wind became an echo. The flowers, those living jewels, were now but a patch of unimportant colour against the green of leaf and tree. As Iesa longed for the unobtainable, she herself had become as unreachable as that which she sought, and this left Ilniah dispossessed, no longer able to see the beauty of the Garden.

As strangeness grew in Ilniah's heart, the seed in Iesa's thoughts finally grew to fruition. At last she spoke. "We have no lasting beauty but this Jewel before us, Ilniah. Though it lights my thoughts and dreams, it is not enough to merely gaze and play. No my given one, the Jewel demands to be grasped, to be taken, to be truly embraced. It's presence is a question in my heart, and my heart demands an answer."

Iesa leapt up without warning. Seeking to grasp the Jewel that shone so true. Yet leap and grasp as she would, just as she came close the Jewel would turn in on itself and shift to a place beyond her reach. Frustration showed on her face. She leapt again and again but never once would the Jewel be caught. The harder she tried the more elusive became the secret before her.

Pain and deep furrows started to crease Ilniah's heart. Why did his beloved act this way? She needed this gem more than she needed him, and now in her panic to grab it she did not even notice how she was crushing the flowers and destroying the Garden around her. Each moment began to break up into a staccato series of images that swirled the emotions and grew this frightening sense of confusion.

The birds stopped singing, the blades of grass stopped whispering to the wind, and the song of life itself seemed to stop flowing. Needing something to hold onto, Ilniah struck out against this darkness that was forming in his mind. Physically he grasped and threw his beloved to the ground, saying "Stop your foolish dreams my chosen! Come be with me once more, share the joy of our hearts!"

Iesa recoiled from him by instinct, and twisting like a cat she whipped up and around him, and away from his grasp. She cried out "How dare you seek to possess me!" Her words were an accusing dagger thrown at her once beloved, the one who now writhed with pain and anguish for what has been lost.

"What right have you to take me from my chosen path? You are worse than this accursed Jewel that taunts and dances before my eyes. At least it leaves me free, but you! You would hold me down and ignore my dream. You would bar my freedom! Leave me Ilniah. Leave me alone! Leave me be." And with these harsh words she turned with her back as an answer to the doubts and suffering in his thoughts. Her sharp words cut the perfection of his love, and he wept, feeling a vast chasm opening up into which his heart fell.

His love was so bereft that he could not fight back. Even in pain and torment he could say nothing, for now he knew the fear of separation. He feared that more words might lead to the ending of all that had been between them. He wanted to stop her, hold her down, it was true. He wanted to have her for himself. He wanted her to see the foolishness of her dream. He wanted things to go back to how they were. Yet inside he knew it would never be the same again.

In silence he picked up his broken dreams and walked away, leaving the fragments of his very being trailing like a lost dog behind. Empty of life, devoid of emotion, Ilniah walked into the dense foliage of the wild forest that surrounded the Garden. A leaf cast loose from the tree. The Garden watched impassively as it saw the two lovers part, looking with hopeless hope into their Souls for the answer to their needs.

Ilniah's Journey

For a lifetime, an eternity, he wandered confused. The span of lost memories was the road upon which Ilniah walked. Aimlessness was his only goal, even as it was his jail. No dream inspired him and anything he did reminded him of loss, the empty space in his heart into where all his wishes had fallen. No longer did he delight in the grass underfoot or the song of the birds. No more did he explore the endless textures of God's creation nor seek anything but the misery of his life at every turn.

His nose no longer recognised the sweet scent of the blooms, his mind no longer felt the passing of the moments for all seemed to be caught in an endless drudge. He knew nothing, could understand nothing, other than the fact that joy had left and misery had taken over his house.

This Jewel his Love sought to capture: What was it that called her so fiercely, and caused her to despise him? Empty dreams echoed, with no reply.

Cold existed in the deep forest, and there were animals that did not delight in existence, but looked to eat it. Ilniah had to take care lest he become a meal for a passing tiger or bear, and he needed to find covering for his body at night, or else he shivered in the cold. High in the trees he would climb up to where monkeys would chatter and argue, but eventually they accepted him and allowed him to rest with them at nights. It was company of sorts and over time, he found their ways not unkind, and the fruits they ate satisfying to his hunger.

Wisdom came to him like a cat on silent feet. He watched the monkeys fight and make friends in circles of discontent and content, and he started wondering if the deep hurt he felt from Iesa was not just something natural, like what he experienced here in the deep forest. He still did not understand why she was so possessed by the Jewel, but he found himself more allowing of her needs.

The sense of uselessness began to fade, and the pain became a memory as over time Ilniah began to find a sense of being outside of the Garden. There was something enlivening about the danger of the woods. Your heart was alive and attuned to the passing of time and your ears listened for danger. Yet at the same time, there was an electric sense that came from the possibility of being eaten that thrilled him.

He could pick up sticks and throw stones to frighten away predators, and the monkey people came to respect him. He also taught them how to use a forked branch to reach for fruit that was hard to get. They knew he was not one of them, yet this strange addition to their tribe was useful.

Within their simple acceptance Ilniah felt his pain evaporate, and over time it became as a mist over the lake. It was still there, yet less real. "I am alone," he said to himself. "But I need not be lonely"

This revelation became as a rock upon which he could stand. It had an immutable strength from which he could draw and a joy long forgotten began to flow back into his veins. All his inner tears became a wellspring, and his pain melted to form a nectar sweet to the lips of his being. As if born again, the subtle flavours of the world about him seemed to return, flowing back into the river of continuity, taking him on the journey of Love.

The re-birth of joy took root in his soul, and it called him. Gazing within, Ilniah felt a rush of knowingness, something certain in the infinite mystery of life and living once more came to his heart and blessed the rock upon which he stood.

"I am alone, yet I need not be lonely!" Somehow the importance of the words reached his mind, and he knew it was time to seek out Iesa. Now he knew for certain that he loved her, whereas before he just presumed it. The period apart had given him a strength of being, a sense of purpose. Just as he had helped his Monkey Brothers he might also be able to help his beloved.

If she still needed to catch this jewel, perhaps he could help her? After all, her search had forced him to begin his, and in finding his truth he was set more free than he had ever been. For the first time in his existence he had been USEFUL and there was no flavour or scent or texture in all of God's garden that could equal this inner sense of being.

The aether about him seemed to part, as veils held long before his eyes started to fall away. It is true, it had been a wonderful dream in the Garden, but looking back he had only been half alive. Perhaps this was the journey that Iesa needed to take, but she was doing it in her own way. It was not for him to decide what was right or wrong for her, but if he truly cared, he would help. Or at least, offer his help.

If she rejected him again, he had his friends in the jungle he could go back to. And so, secure in his own presence, Ilniah made his way back to the Eternal Garden. But what a shock greeted him!

Weeds had taken over the flower beds, the fruit hung rotten on the trees, and a smell of decay was everywhere. After the fresh, damp air of the forest it seemed impassively hot and clammy. Was this the place of joy he remembered in his thoughts? But in the distance a familiar hum reached his ears, and he followed it to its source.

As he made his way through the vines and underbrush, he pushed into a clearing where the Garden still remained, and there before him was the radiant Jewel of Truth. How could he have forgotten this indescribable joy? The rays of light that shone from this wondrous creation filled his heart with light and his mind with clarity, but now there was no fog clouding him. For the first time he saw the true brilliance of this ancient thing. Deeply did he drink of its infinite ambrosia, feeling it flow into every atom of his being like rain soaking into the parched deserts.

The wine of God is heady and strong, yet the hardened soul that had survived the forest and served his brothers could absorb its powerful lustre. He realised that everything that was broken was mended: This was IT! This was the forever moment, unbroken, untarnished and indescribable.

The Jewel seemed to come closer and closer, and then without warning it entered into his very being, into his heart, into his mind, into his Soul. A wind rushed through his being, but it was nothing. It was an emptiness so utterly profound, yet a completion that was totally complete. There were no words or feeling that could give the secret this blessing of the jewel gave, yet it was both everything and nothing, high and low, gentle yet ruthless.

It seemed perfect, but the energy just kept building until it was all he could do to hold his heart from exploding. With no warning, a surge of pure joy passed through him, yet it came as a great shock that rattled the very atoms of his being. Was this death? Had he taken too much? And then, nothing.

Eternity itself may have passed him by, and he would have known nothing. All was a deafening silent to Ilniah, and yet some part of himself knew he still continued. Was this the life after? A whispering murmur came into his thoughts, more like the wind than a voice. "This is truth" it seemed to say. But it seemed a hollow drum.

With this thought a beating sound drew his attention, ka-thump, ka-thump it went. Slowly he realised it was the beating of his own heart. With a gasp he took in a shock of air and opened his eyes to find himself on his back, lying on the grass in the Garden. Over him and on bended knee was Iesa.

She looked half mad. Her hair had not been combed in months, and she appeared like one of the wild animals he had been living with. She shook him. "The Jewel! You saw the jewel!" she demanded. "It came to you. It came INTO you!"

A great sense of compassion came over Ilniah. He said "You are my Jewel, beloved."

She screamed, a scream filled with angst and frustration, and he knew that her mind had been bent by the power of the Jewel of Truth. Even as he knew why it had selected him, he could also understand why it had let Iesa alone. She had not understood the wild world, nor lived outside the safe confines of the Garden. The sheer wildness of the Jewel is something you have to be prepared for, or else it would destroy you with its power.

He knew better than to try and hold her. She had become an animal and neither reason nor love would tempt her to stay, so with great sadness he watched her run off into the forest. He hoped she would be safe, that she would survive, and he hoped that one day she might return. But for now there was a garden than needed tending, a home to rebuild.

For a long time he worked. Weeding, clearing the overgrown areas, clearing up the flower beds. Odd, he thought to himself, how once it all just seemed to look after itself. But it was no matter. He enjoyed his work and enjoyed his monkey friends who came to to visit for the fruits and other morsels he put out for them. They had once held a great fear of this place, and he supposed it was the Jewel.

Of course, now he knew why there was eternal day here. The light of the Jewel was a perpetual candle. As he worked to clear things, he started to see how the jewel itself grew stronger. It was as if it fed the garden, yet the garden fed it. It stayed near him as he worked and became a constant companion until in the fullness of time the Garden itself was restored.

But now it was so much more, because he had brought the monkeys and they had brought other curious animals, and now even the Tiger would sit on the perimeter apparently mesmerised by the beautiful light and sound emanating from its heart.

Slowly too other changes happened. As the Garden came back to itself, the wild child that was Iesa seemed to calm down. She sat for periods at the edge, like the wild animals, but over time she came closer. He gave her fruit and nectar, and quietly smiled whenever she came near. She still glanced up hesitatingly at the Jewel, but she no longer stared at it endlessly, and she no longer sought to pursue it.

Then one day, Iesa brought him a gift. A small offering, yes, but a gift is so important that it matters not what it is, only the spirit in which it is given. She laid before him one of the wild flowers, and with it some seeds.

Ah, so perfect! This is what the Garden needed. Some of the wild energy from the forest needed to become part of it. So he smiled, thanked her, and asked that she collect whatever things of beauty that she found, and that they could bring this into the Garden to make it complete.

Day by day, moment by moment, they started to work together, planting the seeds, weeding the soil and giving out the extra harvest to the animals that came for food. It took a great deal of time, but eventually Iesa learned to smile again, and finally she began to laugh. And at last, at last she began to speak.

"I was very glad you were alive," she said, "Yet at the same time, seeing you catch the jewel so easily after all the efforts I had made, I became so jealous that my mind refused to believe it. I hated you, and I hated myself for this.

"Then I left and intended to never come back, but the song of the Garden grew stronger, and I had to see why. That's when I saw you working every day. I would come to watch you, and I started to remember the times we shared. I began to feel ashamed, and hid again in the forest, but then one day a beautiful flower, one I had never seen before was in front of me. In the deep forest, where I had never gone, there were these wonderful flowers.

"I knew they would love being here in the Eternal Garden, so I brought you one. Because you could accept the flower and its wildness, I started to believe again. I am not sure what I believed in, but something started to wake up. I still have a pain, because you found the Jewel and not I, but now I find joy in the simple things again, and the pain is less."

Ilniah stopped what he was doing, and looked deeply at his beloved. "You are my Jewel. This is your Home. I suffered with the loss of your joy, but I found myself because of it. I have learned to serve life rather than take from it, and this is the simple truth the jewel has given me. And now you too serve the Garden, and the animals, and the forest.

"We are no longer the children that played without care or concern for our world, but it took your pursuit of the Jewel to shake me from my sleep. So you have been the true cause of everything I have become, not the jewel.

"Beloved Iesa, YOU are my Jewel. You are my Light. You are my journey, my home, my path, my food, and my wine."

With tears flowing from her eyes, she embraced him. "You are my very Soul, Ilniah. I am so sorry for hurting you." The music of the Garden, like the nectar of truth itself, once more flowed through the air and wrapped them as the both wept.

Iesa looked up to gaze into her love's eyes, and to her surprise, the Jewel she had so long sought was somehow there. It was the Light of Love and like the blessing of God itself, it moved imperceptibly into their midst.

"Alone but not lonely," it whispered to her, and at last, she understood.

A Meeting of True Hearts

I am used to the forest. I know its ways, and I can feel a shift in the air about me when something or someone approaches. Like all things that live, there is a message stick that is sent out with each change, and you only have to remain aware enough to read the signs and know the ways.

As a child, I was shown by some aboriginal boys, who were boarding at a school I went to, some of their bush tricks. How to sing up a fish; how to whistle a fox; how to smell out water, etc. What signs the ants make when it is going to rain becomes as clear and easy as reading a book when you know what to look for. In my life I was rarely surprised, because even in the world of social confusion, the signals of change are still there.

That was what surprised me the most, the way he first appeared with no hint, no warning. Yet, while so vulnerable and small, he seemed completely composed. While so apparently unprepared for the wild, with nothing but himself, somehow he seemed to have no trouble surviving here.

And the lad continued to surprise, and delight, me. The story of the garden and the jewel was a beautiful tale, and we discussed it long into the night. I once had a love I had lost, which is what I presumed his flower really was, so I felt we had common ground. Yet for the life of me, it really did feel as if I was sitting and talking with a person who came from another planet.

The boy was always polite and in his way courteous, yet he remained so very distant that, on occasions, I wondered if he even knew I was here. Then he would stop, and look directly at me with those pale, sea green eyes, and every time he did this it was as if my heart was nailed to the spot. Perhaps he really was a prince?

We got on well, and I was very glad for his company. I started to see that it was not so much people I disliked and Nature that I preferred, but simply that most people just do not want to talk about things I found interesting. It's not their fault, nor is it mine, it is just that we do not find common ground. Yet here, with this strange child, I had a friend. I found it so easy talking with him, which only highlighted how difficult it was when I tried to get along with others.

For most people communication is really competition. Who is brighter, quicker, sharper, slicker, and behind the back of our so-called friends, we snicker about their shortcomings to our other friends. It's a thing that tires me, but with this odd child, I felt enlivened, looking forward to whatever came up next. And yet I also felt oddly insecure. It's odd, I know, but that was just how it was.

After he finished his tale about the Garden we got back to his visit with the Gardener.

"I woke up that morning and told the old man of the dream I had. He found it very interesting because when he had first come to this place one of the old men that lived there spoke about how this area we were standing in was once locally known as the Eternal Garden, but he knew nothing of Ilniah or Iesa.

"He gave me a piece of paper with writing on it, and on it was a riddle, or at least he said it was a riddle."

"What did it say?" I asked.

The boy stopped and shuffled around his yellow, oversize coat, and pulled from one of the pockets something that looked like a role of parchment. "Here, read it for yourself" he said.

I opened up the small role, and on it were some weird hieroglyphs, like nothing I had ever seen before. "I can't read this language, I am so sorry. This is what the Gardener gave you?"

"Oh yes!" he said "I can't read it either, which is why the Gardener gave me this special glass. You look through it to see what is really there."

I took from him this odd, oval shaped object that looked like a small hand mirror, only there was a milky yellow translucent stone where the mirror would have been. It was quite extraordinary, and like nothing I had ever seen, but what it did was even more remarkable. When I held it over the strange script, I saw pictures in the translucent stone.

A butterfly landed beside a caterpillar, and said something. The caterpillar turns around and falls over. It was very different, oddly funny, and strikingly old in a way I could not explain. "Do you remember what the Gardener said about the story?" I asked.

"It was a rhyming riddle that went:"

A Butterfly one day flying through

Saw a Caterpillar it thought it knew.

So they stopped and chatted about the day

But before they were about to go their way

Butterfly asked, "So many legs and all

How do you walk and not somehow fall?

The caterpillar wondered and looked back to spy

But he looked too hard and he went all awry

This happened long, long ago

But really, it still pays to know

What a foolish thing we will do

When we start to think "me" instead of "you"

I laughed. It was an old story, but the message remains so true. We all just get along fine, but someone stops and asks us about the details of our life, and we stumble. "I think I like your Gardener," I said.

The boy laughed, he had a wonderful open full hearted laugh, but then he grew serious again. "There IS a real Jewel, isn't there? I know it may have been just a dream, but something tells me there is more, and you seem to know about jewels."

I started to see part of his reason for being here was because I had shown him some jewels. Well, that was fair enough, he told me stories so I could spend some time talking about gemstones. "There are many different types of Jewels. I see them in rocks, of course, but I also see them in the heart of a happy soul. A diamond can gleam brightly and reflect the light of the sun, but so too can the face of a child, or the eyes of a person that loves you. Even the water on the lake can sparkle like a jewel, but it can fade so easily. Yet when someone loves you, well, this is a forever thing.

"For me there is a Jewel of Truth in every sunrise, in every bird that sings its simple song for the sheer love of singing. These are moment when I feel a priceless gift of love in my Soul, these are times when I am able to embrace life wholeheartedly. Like when I first got to this lake, I felt wonderful. Do you think that maybe THIS might be the jewel?"

He was quiet for a considerable length of time, and stood there just watching as I stoked up the fire for a pot of tea. The evening was upon us once more. Finally he spoke, as we sat watching the sunset. "I think that what the Gardener was trying to tell me is that the beauty of life is always before us, but that we can not truly hold it in our hearts until we discover this same beauty within us."

The fire danced and crackled, and the cool of the evening came to settle any debt we owned to conversation. Silence filled the moments so perfectly, I did not want to disturb her, so I quietly went about the camp tasks, making a soup for us, and breaking some bread we could sop it with. I was very tired, and wrapped a blanket around our young soul, and slipped off into my own world of dreams, smiling within and I flew away on the wings of peace.

Oooo0000oooO

Judging by the lilt in his step he had been awake for some time. I was still struggling to defeat sleep and arise like the butterfly from my cocoon. It was early and the sun carried very little heat, so I prodded the fire to life, and put on some tea. We sat to drink, and the lad continued with his tale of the night before.

"I left the old man to his Garden, for our words were done. Soon I found this magnificent highway that opened up before me. It was of fine cobblestones that had been smoothed over by years of traffic. Flowers grew wild, and every hundred steps you would smell something different and unique. Splendid rainbows would reach out from the horizon and stretch across the sky and passing clouds would take shapes and forms as if they were playing a game between themselves.

I tried to catch some of the smaller rainbows that reached out near me, but they were shy creatures and ran away. Which is perhaps for the best, because so often what seems a delight in the distance become ordinary and common place when we have it in our hand.

"Soon I came across a man, and he seemed exceedingly odd against this landscape of dreams. He walked briskly, with no time for the world about him. He had a very grey, serious face, and he clearly had no time for anything but the matters of importance in his thoughts. He saw nothing of what was around him, or if he did he paid it no attention.

"He was tall and gangly, with fright-filled eyes that seemed possessed with some sort of secret that I could not fathom. I do not believe he noticed anything about himself at all, least of all myself.

"What was so very odd was that the man carried a huge cardboard box, and almost ran into me while muttering to himself words I could not understand. I had to call out to him 'Excuse me!' or he would have surely walked right into me.

The Box Man

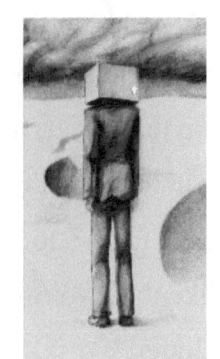

What what WHAT!" the man exclaimed. "Who is trying to destroy my life. What vicious creature is out to kill me!" The man dropped his box with the panic, then looked even more panicked as he saw his box hit the ground. "Nooo! Noooo, not my box! How awful, how shocking, how indescribably terrible a day this is becoming."

Then he saw the small child who had frightened him. "Horrid creature, what right have you got to scare decent citizens like this? Who gave you the right to accost innocent men as they walk down the highway? I have a good mind to sue you for damages, and fright, you nasty wicked boy. I suppose you think you are very clever doing this to an old man, hey? Don't you?"

"Forgive me if I have upset you, Sir, but you were just about to walk into me. I do hope that nothing in your box has been broken."

The man glared. "Anything broken?" he snorted. "First you purposely scare me, now you insult me, you whipper snapper. You young imp, of course nothing is broken. How dare you suggest I would sully me beautiful box with THINGS. What a low suggestion, what a callous child. Break anything indeed! Hurrumph."

I looked up at the man, wondering what on earth he was talking about. The fellow seemed completely mad, but to suggest his box is better with nothing in it? It seemed very strange. Then the man continued, as if to himself.

"Not that I haven't been tempted. Yes indeed I have been tempted. You think that maybe that small little packet of tissues could go in the box, and that would make your life easier. But would it, really? Easier is not easier when you know you have defiled your box. Oh no, I don't put anything in it, nothing, not a thing. My box is pure and unadulterated. Anything that could be broken? No, certainly not. I have worked too hard for too long to ruin my reputation by falling to a lurid temptation like this. No my box is completely free of all forms of unnecessary clutter."

"Forgive me for asking, but I am now very curious as to why you would want to carry around an empty box. It does seem odd." I questioned.

"Why carry an empty box? Why carry an empty BOX?" The man looked incredulous. "Have you no idea at all about important things? I mean, have you no imagination? How many uses are there for an empty box? Thousands and thousands of uses, and therefore a man with that empty box is ALSO very useful, and therefore very important. Not only is an empty box important, it is very easy to carry because it is light weight and naturally the larger the empty box you carry, the greater potential you have to putting useful things in it. In fact, my box is so large that if I left the top open I could fit an enormous number of things in it. Possibly one very big thing and a few other smaller things, or, or, or maybe a batch of tiny things as well. What do you think about THAT, you young imp?"

"If I understand you, what you are carrying about is your potential to be useful? Is this the only reason you carry around such a large box, or is there some other use besides it's potential?"

"I see you are perhaps a little wiser than I first gave you credit for, child. How right you are, how right you are. This is a very worthwhile and worthy question, because it must be clear to you by now that only men of high standing and powerful moral fibre can resist the temptation of ruining their potential by filling their box with stuff.

"Why, most men you meet wander around aimlessly, carry nothing of worth and walk about empty handed. Empty headed as well, I dare say, eh what? Ha! Yes indeed, funny pun that. Clearly because I have a box, I have potential. Also, because my hands are kept busy, I am not causing trouble. If I am not causing trouble, given the state of society today, I am therefore a veritable boon to society. All this is demonstrated not just by my box, but by its emptiness! You see? Of course you can. So you can now see how incredibly important my box is, can't you?

"And what's more, besides being a useful box, no one has claim to it but myself. It is all mine, all my own and no-one but myself has the right to carry it. This is a worthy thing, a thing to be proud of, don't you think?"

"Oh I do," I said, not wanting to aggravate the man any further. "I see things clearly now, but at least allow me to show you a way to carry your wonderful box more easily. Would you like to see this?"

The man looked instantly suspicious. "You are not going to be nasty and put something in my beautiful box, are you?"

"Absolutely not" I answered. "I just want to show you a trick I learned that makes carrying an empty box very easy, and a lot safer because you will also be able to see where you are going."

"Yes, well. Perhaps this might be alright," said the man, cautiously. He was very suspicious of the child, but if he could manage to carry this enormous box more easily, then maybe he might also be able to find an even bigger one that he might carry around. That would be nice.

I then went up to the box, which was in reality a large white cardboard one that we might commonly call a packing box, and I simply flipped up the inserts (which allowed the box to fold flat) then handed it back to the man. Obviously I expected that the man would be pleased with such a labour saving to himself, but instead the fellow was horrified!

"Oh my goodness! Oh my socks are burning!" the man exclaimed. "What have you done to my beautiful box! You have made it all completely flat and USELESS. What a disgrace! What will my neighbours think? They will look at me and laugh, saying I am nothing, a no one, and not worth a moments notice!" and with this the man broke down into inconsolable sobbing. "Ruined. I am utterly ruined!" he wailed.

Trying to put things right, I hurriedly put the box back together again, back the way it was, saying, "Look! See? Your box is back now. "

This unfortunately had a far worse effect on the man than the collapsing of the cardboard. "You horrendous little thug!" he shouted. "As if it was not enough to destroy my whole sense of self-worth, now you are mocking me. You are trying to convince me that the Box I had so highly prized for its usefulness is worthless, mere cardboard! But this flip flop magic you are doing won't convince me, you hear. It's just tricks, I know it is!

"You cruel and thoughtless child, seeking to ruin my life, taking away everything I prize with your glib cleverness. But how can I go amongst my fellows now, knowing that at any moment my beautiful, wonderful box might collapse into a mere flat nothing. I can never be seen in public again. The shame, the horror, the evil of it all is too much. I hate you, you hear! I absolutely loath and detest you!" Whereupon the fellow collapsed into helpless, weeping rage, drumming his hands on the ground, while alternatively reaching out to caress his newly reformed box.

What could I do? I had meant well, but everything I did made things worse. It seemed to me that the real problem was that the man didn't have anything in his life but his box, so I made a suggestion. "Sir, I am very sorry for the upset this has caused. Perhaps you would allow me to show you a way that your box could be returned to its former stature, and be a thing of great value once more. Because if we could do this, you would see that your life has not been wasted and that there has been a purpose for carrying your box for so long. Would you like to try this?"

He looked up with one eye brow raised, and stopping the weeping for a moment, he looked interested. "You could do this?" he asked, dabbing his eyes with a handkerchief he had found. "Could you really show me how to find a worthwhile purpose for my box?"

"I think so," I answered. So I asked him, "Are there any areas along this highway where there are no beautiful flowers, places that are a little ugly?"

"Well yes. But I can't see what this has to do with my box" he answered.

"It's very simple, and it is something everyone can talk about, and say how wonderful you are after you have done it. All you have to do is to collect some of the flowers that grow here, and transplant them to one of the ugly parts of the road. By using your box to help move flowers and beautiful things, everything will then serve a useful purpose and people can then talk about the marvellous man with the big box who did this wonderful job that made everyone's life better."

"WHAT!" he shouted. "Dirty up my beautiful box with filthy little miserable and insignificant flowers? What a despicable mind you have, what a horrid creature you are. What a terrible thing to say to my beautiful box!

"No thank you Sir!" he said gathering up both his box and his pride. "No thank you. I will find a proper purpose for MY box, if you don't mind. And it will be something of worth, not mere piddling snap dragons and the like. Good day to you Sir, you scamp, you noisesome troublemaker, and I pray that I will never have the misfortune of having to meet your sorry self ever again." And with this he huffed off indignantly down the road, stroking and patting his box as if to cure it of the injury it has just suffered.

I called out after him "Flowers are NOT insignificant and worthless!" but I was speaking to myself. He would have no more of me. This was a sad thing, I thought, for his box could have been very useful but now both must travel to their destiny as useless potential. Fortunately I had no such burden to bear, but neither did I exactly know what I was doing or where I was going. In this sense, my thoughts were like his empty box. I had to carry them, but I had no idea what to do with them.

He looked up. The story had clearly ended, so I ventured a comment. "Perhaps this is why we met, so you could give your thoughts to me?"

"Perhaps," he said. "It is so hard to know even the smallest thing for certain, let alone what you must do with it in order to make it useful." He and I turned to gaze out over the Lake, watching the rising moon play it like a fiddle. The dancing light seemed to almost hypnotise us, and silence ruled for some time. Finally the boy added, supposedly to me, but really to himself. "I can only suppose that we must hope to see the obvious one day. That's what the Turtle said, that if it is not already obvious then it isn't worth it."

"Turtle?" I asked … "What Turtle?"

The Riddle Turtle

It was living in a lake that was beside the road, near where I had just left the Box Man. I must have looked confused, because as I sat there washing my face, I heard it speak to me. "BY ZEUS!" it said, but not aloud. I heard it inside me. I looked about and could see nothing, but then a pair of eyes appeared out of the water.

"It was a turtle, and it was looking directly at me. At first I had no idea it was a talking turtle, of course, and the reason I spoke to it was simply because I always speak to animals that seem nice. I never expect them to understand, but I talk to them to show I am being friendly and would not seek to harm them. Which is why I said 'Hello!' to this turtle."

"Hello" it answered back.

"I was much surprised, and very taken aback, though I shouldn't be because, after all, I had a rose that spoke to me. But here and now it was most unexpected, and I really had no idea what next to say. I am supposing that the Turtle was expecting me to say something, because he just stayed there, with his head out of the water, looking at me."

"Hello" I said again, "Lovely weather isn't it."

"Hmmmm," said the turtle. "Weather in a lake is more a question of bright or dull, and either or neither is fine."

Naturally there was a long pause. This was not exactly an invitation to talk, but neither was it a hint to not talk. It was probably just one of those spaces where with a little effort two different creatures can find common ground, but at first you never know. "Or dark?" I suggested. "You could have bright, dull, or dark."

Once again the Turtle just looked, taking its time. "Wet and dry has no in-between." It simply said "but daylight has many shades and textures, as does dark. My concern is not the influence without, but the fluency within."

I stopped and had to think about this play on words. It is quite true, wet or dry has no in-between, but as to the rest it seemed just words. However he seemed a very nice turtle, so I asked him, "Have you lived here for a long time?"

"Have you every wondered how short a thing time is for a plant, yet so long for a tree, and how incredibly long it must be for a rock?" One must suppose that for a turtle, time has an entirely different perspective, but this was a very different way of looking at things. It possibly noticed my puzzled look, because it continued, "The longest time is a place where there is no time. For a bird, that flies so fast, it looks down on myself, and my turtle time flows so slowly. But for a plant, it looks out to see me, and my turtle time is fast. For a rock we are all incredibly swift, and passing, and fragile."

It was going to be difficult talking with this creature, as you can already guess. "Ah, perhaps you might be able to let me know what lies ahead on this road?"

The turtle laughed a turtle sort of laugh, which was more of a sort of "huff huff huff huff". "There is a road, to be certain. As to what lies on it depends on what choices we have. The choices we have depend on HOW we see, not what we see. And finding the right way is found in asking the right questions. So how to ask the right question is your answer."

Perhaps this was a Riddle Turtle? The answer to a riddle is always simple when you see it, but seeing it is the hard part, Rather than ask a thousand more questions, I asked, "So what is the right question to ask?"

"That is the question." The turtle nodded quite sombrely, and agreed.

Then he just stopped, saying nothing. I waited for quite some time, but he said nothing more. Finally I asked "Well, do you know the answer?"

"If it's not obvious, it's not worth it." And with this the Riddle Turtle slid its head back down under the water, and I never saw him again.

The child looked up, after acting out this story as a pantomime for me, and asked "What do you imagine the Turtle meant by this?"

It was quite a puzzle, and truth to say, I wasn't sure. Maybe the turtle was just mad, or had spent too long in his own thoughts and they no longer connected up with the rest of the world. Yet in my world there was a thing called "Occam's Razor" which is a way to say that the most obvious, most simple explanation is often the correct one. "Well, the turtle did say that the road ahead depends on your choices, and I know that the choices I make really do depend on how I am seeing things at the time. I often look back at silly choices I have made, and in retrospect it is very obvious they were not very smart. Yet at the time it seemed the right thing to do. However if I had been able to see the obvious I would have saved myself a good deal of time and trouble."

I paused, and he looked out over the lake. Finally he spoke.

"It was obvious to me that I didn't make wise decisions regarding my Rose, yet could I have decided anything other than I could at the time? This seems more of the right sort of question, because the simple truth is that we can only do what we can do. When I started to understand this I felt the pain in my heart lessen.

"This then was the obvious, that I had suffered for what I did not know."

It was difficult for me to get my head around this, but it started to make sense. When I thought of all the time I had wasted in uphill battles over what amounted to nothing. In the end, it was obvious that it was a waste of time, but because I now knew it was a waste, the time wasn't entirely wasted. "Do you think the Turtle was really talking about wisdom?" I offered. "It seemed to me that the Turtle was speaking about seeing things simply, seeing things as they are, and not as we imagine. Perhaps this is what makes the road ahead?"

"It was a Riddle Turtle," said the boy, simply. "What he said was only half the puzzle, HOW he said it was the other half."

"And how did he say it?" I asked.

"Kindly. He seemed so very kind" he said as he gazed off once more into the distance. "And that is what made him so wise."

There was one other small thing, an odd comment that stayed in my thoughts that seemed to be something else the Riddle Turtle had said: *This Moment. It is something Time calls its own, just before it loses it forever. But to a Moment, what is a Time?*

After some time, listening to the sound of night all around, he spoke about a strange race he met further along the road, a folk he called the "Ladder Men".

The Ladder Men

As I walked down the road I came onto a vast open field that had great mountains as their backdrop. It was a very beautiful place, but I could see a lot of activity with people shouting, and orders being given, and things pushed about with a great sense of rush. Over to the side I could see a small village. I was curious about what the workmen were doing in the field, so I stepped off the road to take a closer look. It turns out they were all busy making ladders."

"Ladders?" I asked. "That seems an odd thing for people to make out in the country. How many people were there?" I asked.

"Oh, a good 40 or more men were building the ladders, but there would have been over a hundred doing various tasks connected with ladder building. Some men were using an adze to trim the raw timer, other were boiling and steaming the wood to make it pliable, still others were sharpening tools. It was quite an industrial complex .

"And they made all sorts of ladders. Wide ones that many people could climb, short ones of just two steps, two sided ladders, three sided ladders, four sided ladders, even ROUND ladders!"

"Round Ladders? That seems very odd."

"Exactly my thoughts, which is why I went up to ask what anyone would want a round ladder for ."

ooooo0000oooo

"Excuse me, but may I ask what you are doing out in this field building round ladders?" I asked to the worker who seemed less occupied than some of his fellows.

"What are we doing building ladders?" he said, laughing. "Well I would have thought this was terribly obvious, wouldn't you? It is a very stupid question as it answers itself." Then looking over his shoulder to another man, the fellow called out, "Hey listen up, this little rascal wants to know what we are doing in a field building ladders!"

"My goodness, they're not growing them smarter and smarter now-a-days are they? What are we doing building ladders, I mean, do you suppose we are really building ballet shoes, hey?" the men laughed at the child, but otherwise just went about their business and ignored him.

"I must say" said the child to me as he told the tale. "At this point I was very annoyed, not just because they were right and it was not a good question, but I was annoyed because I was getting annoyed. I had to swallow my pride to ask the question I really wanted to ask."

"What I am asking is what point does all this ladder building achieve? Does it serve a purpose because as far as I can see, the village over there does not have enough people to support a ladder building industry."

The two men looked at each other, stopped their sarcasm for a moment, and one winked at the other. "Yes, well this is an astute question because it takes into account the demographics of the situation, but let me assure you, we have looked into this and have found that the ladder building industry is economically viable, ecologically reasonable and ergonomically practical."

The other man, the one who was building round ladders, chirped in. "Indeed, the nature of the commercial endeavour, as witnessed by your good self, is a suitable and financially rewarding stimulus that aggregates the sum finances of the said villagers into a very well defined class. Ergo: We are Traders, they are Buyers."

There is an old rule of thumb in life, and that is when someone is using too many words to describe something that seems obvious, then those words are hiding something that is not being said.

"Look," the child said, "I have travelled to many places, and I have never seen so many people building so many different types of ladders for so few people. A person will buy one ladder, and it is to get to somewhere they usually cannot reach. But once they own a ladder, they don't need another one for a very long time. Now if there are 40 ladder makers in a field outside a town where there looks to be less than 1000 people, I divide 40 into 1000 and get 25. That's 25 people to every ladder maker. Even if you built only one ladder each week there are 52 weeks in the year and people do not need a new ladder twice a year."

"Can't argue with the math," said the Round Ladder man. "Only we do not sell our ladders! Oh no, they are far too valuable to sell. They never leave this field."

The child was incredulous. This made no sense at all. "Then why do you build ladders, if you don't let them leave the field and especially if you don't sell them."

"Ah HA!" said the man's friend, who was putting finishing touches to his four sided ladder. "Exactly! Because we do not allow them to leave the field, if the villagers wish to experience the sublime joy and pleasure of our ladders, they must come to US. And of course, they all must pay for the great and enormous pleasure of experiencing a Ladder Man ladder."

"People pay you to use a ladder out here in a field? I can't say in understand this at all. It makes no sense to me" said the child. "Ladders are for things you must do around the home, and why would someone pay money to use a ladder in a field, where it serves no purpose?"

"Yes indeed," said a third ladder man who had just finished setting up a three sided ladder and was putting out a sign saying 'Ladder Ride $2.00'. "Purpose is what it is all about, and we Ladder Men serve the highest of all purposes. We help people achieve a different viewpoint."

The round ladder man chimed in. "Indeed, people come out here, downcast and depressed after a hard day of pointless work for too little pay, and they cheer up as soon as they see us. Why? Because we improve their life."

The Four Sided Ladder man continued, "We improve their life because we give them the opportunity to rise above their worldly concerns and achieve a sense of being above it all. The villagers come out here, pay their money and every day they can experience a new high, a different ladder for every mood they may have."

The child looked at me, saying "There was a problem in my thoughts here, because it sounded so reasonable, yet was obviously so absurd. But I had it in mind to find out more before I moved on that day, because while it seemed impossible, it also seemed to hold something important. So I asked further."

"Well, people come out to these ladders to improve their day. I can understand this, it's a sort of amusement park. But what happens? I mean they climb a ladder, get a higher view, but then they have to come back down to the same world they thought they had risen above."

"Amusement Park?" snorted the Round Ladder man. "I should say we are vastly more important than a mere amusement park. Why we lift the people's spirit, and give them hope that the next day will be worth completing, because then they can come out to us and enjoy the heightened viewpoint once more."

"But in the end, they climb up the ladder, and they climb down. That's it really, isn't it?" The child pushed the men to an answer.

"Of course they come back down, said the Four Sided Ladder man. "You would hardly be comfortable sleeping on a ladder, would you? Of course, I did build a ladder once with a bed at the top and it was very popular, but in the end people still had to come down and go to work."

"But this makes no sense at all," the exasperated child said. "Why climb a ladder in order to have to get back down? Really, if someone wanted a higher view, why don't they pack a change of clothes and some lunch, and go hiking up the high mountains in the distance. You can get a much higher viewpoint from the top of a mountain than any ladder can provide."

"Yes my dear friend," the round ladder man said in a conciliatory tone. "It certainly appears madness on the surface, but there is a simple thing you have overlooked. These poor people have jobs that consume long hours, and they just do not have time, with work, and family, and social commitments to just up and leave and go to mountains in the distance. Time is too precious a thing to waste and so we, the ladder men, provide the villagers with cost effective and time proven strategies for any poor worker to escape the humdrum of their existence, while still being connected to the safety of regular work and family. And all this for such a small fee."

"I might add that you look as if you could do with a lift?" hummed the three sided ladder man.

"I don't have any money," the child said, getting ready to leave these strange people.

"You see, there you have it. You have the freedom to travel because you are poor. Our villagers are rich and so they must stay put, thus we give them the pleasure of our ladders and all are made happy," beamed the Round Ladder man.

"Sadly, such is the price of freedom," said the three sided ladder man, with the four sided builder nodding in agreement.

"But freedom costs nothing" the child snapped back, annoyed at their smug attitude.

"Exactly," echoed all three men, "Which is why it is of no value to anyone."

"It's worth a great deal to me!"

"That's only because you have it," came the paradoxical reply. "In fact, because you know it can't be purchased, this is what makes your freedom valuable to yourself, does it not?"

The boy looked at me with those sea green eyes again. "I had to agree in one sense, because it was true. It all seemed so reasonable, and yet so absurd all in the same breath. So I asked them one last question:

"Well, tell me then, I can see why people might pay for the experience of climbing up different ladders, if this is what people like. But why a Round Ladder? It just seems to make no sense at all!"

"Ah yes, the infamous Round Ladder. Very few of us can make these, you know, and they are the greatest of all the ladder men's achievements. Not just because they are so hard to create, but because a person will spend hours climbing my special round ladders, yet never suffer the dissatisfaction of reaching the top and having to come back down again. You see, it can be quite depressing to reach the highest point you can, because the only way after that is down."

The child looked back to from wherever it was his mind went to as he remembered this story. "In the STRANGE logic of the Ladder Men, this made perfect sense. It was not the time to argue the rights or wrongs of things here, but it just seemed sad that so much effort and time and money was being spent on a thing that, in the end, served little true purpose. But I had to suppose that a person getting through their day as best they could was in itself a purpose. With this I went to make my way back to the road and to continue my journey, but the four sided ladder man called me back, saying he wanted to ask me a question."

"I have a question for you young man. It is similar to the type you were asking us, and it is this: What purpose do YOU serve?"

The directness caught the child off guard, and he stumbled a little with his reply. After all, what WAS he doing being free? It was such a sensible sounding question that it seemed like it should be answered, but just at that time the child reached in and felt that piece of paper in his pocket that the Gardener had given him.

"Oh I see" he said to himself "This is the riddle of the Butterfly asking the Caterpillar how he managed to work his legs so well."

"Fortunately," he answered the men "This is something I just do not have to worry about, because I enjoy being free and it causes no one any harm."

"But what PURPOSE does all this freedoms serve?" the round ladder man demanded to know.

"Well, it is useful to me because I have it. It is obviously useless to you, however." he answered.

All three Ladder men looked at each other and nodded, but not in agreement with what the child was saying. "Yes, dangerous words, alright. Just think if all the villagers came out and saw this fellow loitering about? It might put notions in their heads, he might talk about trips up to the mountains. He might even charge to take them there, and that will be money out of our pockets."

The round ladder man continued, "Which would put US out of business!" and looking at the young fellow, he said "I think, young man, that you either tow the line and start paying to climb our ladders, and stop being such a bad influence on everyone, or you move on. You are a terrible example of how to behave, and we do not want to show our villagers your bad habits. You might encourage them to become vagrants and go to the mountains for a higher view."

"But," the child protests, "you said that the reason the villagers were not free to go to the mountains was because they had no TIME! Why then do they waste their time on people like you?"

"Time is a cruel master and we do not question its whim" came the stock reply.

"But you, you who build the ladders. You have lots of time. You could go whenever you wanted and explore more of the world. You are free to do what you will."

"This is true, but we LIKE building ladders." Replied the three sided ladder man. All the men nodded in agreement, causing the coins in their pockets to jingle.

They all looked at me once more, saying in unison, "It's time to move on!" So I made my way back to the road, and, as I climbed out of that valley I heard a siren wail. Looking back to the village I saw hundreds of people streaming out, with eager looks on their faces, all going up to the ladder men, keen to pay for their turn on a ladder."

There were tears in his eyes as he related the last part of the tale. He tried to hold them back, but they escaped despite his best efforts. "Why do people pay the Ladder Men when they get so little in return? Why can people simply not be content, and be free inside their moment?"

I hesitated before answering. Pots so easily call kettles black, and I had spent a lot of time and money on distractions in my life. I really answered myself, as I said "Perhaps we sometimes do not believe we have anything of worth within us to be content with? Perhaps the Ladder Men give the villagers a small sense of accomplishment when their day is otherwise full of failure. I really don't know, but I do know that most people want some sort of good shepherd to guide them, yet equally true, the good shepherd only exists to fleece the flock. And in truth, the flock needs to be shorn or else it is useless"

The child said very little, then after a time he commented, "It's a peculiar state of balance, but there is one thing I felt the Ladder Men really did not grasp."

I waited and let him continue. "They said that my freedom was something that was worthless because it cost nothing, yet in truth, my freedom is something I fought very hard for, and paid a very dear price to have it. I really do not think they even knew what freedom was."

"Perhaps they knew, and perhaps they understood the cost. And perhaps they were just unwilling to pay for it?" I suggested, knowing how many of my school friends were doctors and lawyers, who could be free to do whatever they wanted, but didn't because they felt they had to fulfil the expectations of those around them.

"But freedom is everything!" the child protested.

I looked about in the full bright of the moon, into the stars, and over the lake to the forest. Yes, it really is everything when you have it, but soon I would be going back to the city, looking for new employment, and there was little for it but the slow slavery to something if I were to survive. Ideally I would find something I enjoyed, but the rent had to be paid, so I was pretty uncertain what I would be returning to. I really did understand why people paid the Ladder Men. "Yes, freedom is everything, and yet though you may not understand this as for a little while, one day you might just see that a little slavery is safer. Which reminds me, it's time to eat!"

He sighed a very deep sigh, and just sat there gazing out over the lake while I prepared us some popcorn, firing it up in the camp oven. In a few minutes we were happily munching of lovely hot crunchy popcorn.

Finally he said "It really isn't a choice between slavery and slave master, or walking away, you know. Everyone can be free, it is simply what they choose to do with what they have."

He continued his tale.

The Pillars that Hold up the Sky

Out from the valley of the Ladder Men I walked for quite some time. It was not that the road was deserted, but it was clear that almost no traffic used it, because my company was mostly birds and rabbits. The road was beautifully made, and it also seemed very old and it was paved the whole length with off-white cobble stones. They had been worn by many years, and perhaps centuries, of use.

It was a peculiar place, odd in a way I can not describe other than to say there was a curious song in the air, one that hung like a canvas waiting to be painted on. The day passed quickly, and there were plenty of fruit trees ready to be picked and small streams to drink from. I was puzzled by the complete lack of farming and total lack of people of any sort, but did hear some woodcutters off into the distance.

The road must have led to somewhere, but there were absolutely no markers or signs to show where I was going. I had no idea what lay in store, but as I did not know the way back to my Planet, there was nothing for it but to keep walking, and see what might come of it.

Then the song sharpened, as if saying something was ahead. As I rounded the next bend I came across a huge open space. It was a truly enormous field, and it had the strangest columns set in the middle of it. It was possibly an old temple fallen to ruins, I supposed, and went to have a look.

The road went right past them, so soon I was there in the midst of these huge standing stones, cut from fine marble and standing so tall that

I could not even estimate their height. I marvelled at what incredible things must have existed on this road in the past, yet at the same time I fell into wondering why anyone would build such large pillars and place them into this vast empty space. What was the purpose of it all? I must have said something to myself because I got an answer from somewhere.

"What a stupid question to ask" a large voice came from nowhere, booming across the field and bouncing over the rocks. "It is obvious to any person with but one iota of intelligence why we are here and what we are doing."

"Who… where… what?" I looked about but could see any one. "Hello?" I called out. "Who is there?" The response was not polite.

"Who is there? We are not there, we are here. So are you. Are you completely ignorant, child?" The voice continued to boom and roll over the pasture long after the words had ceased, making it very difficult to focus on where it was coming from.

"Yes," said another deep and powerful voice.  "We work for thousands of years, saving the human race, and then one small-minded human can only manage a 'Gosh who's speaking?' as far as conversation goes. I really wonder why we bother to continue holding up the sky."

I looked to track the source of the great voice, and it seemed to come from the pillars themselves. That was when I realised that they appeared to have a sort of stony face, and then I realised they had eyes that looked down on me. Odd, fabulous and extraordinary as it all may seem, the Pillars themselves seemed to be speaking. "How does a Pillar learn to talk?" I asked out aloud in amazement.

"What? Hurrumph! What do you mean, how does a pillar learn to talk! How does a minute speck of a human learn to walk, I might ask. Of course we can talk! Do you think we stand here all day, working so hard, saying NOTHING?"

"Well" I then asked, "Who is it that built you? Was it the same people who built this road? And WHY were you built here, of all places, so far away from any village or settlement?"

The pillar seemed puzzled by the rush of questions. There was a rushing of wind, a brushing sort of sound, and it appeared that all the pillars were conversing on a level far above me. I could not make out the words, but they sounded very important. Finally they answered as a group, and it was quite deafening when they all spoke together. "We are the Pillars and Pillars are not to be questioned."

The ground underneath shook, the leaves in the trees rattled, but the road stood firm. Was that it? Case closed? "Oh come on," I said. "That's not fair, all I wanted to know was a little history and there is no one else around here to ask."

The Main Pillar looked back down, and gruffly said "We do not have time for your silly questions. My hands are quite full of far more important matters, like holding up the sky."

"Well," I continued. "I would have thought that a pillar who could talk was a very important thing all by itself. I know that in all my life I have never seen a stone pillar who could talk, and if I knew a little more about you I could then tell others about this amazing creation on this extraordinary road that was so far from anywhere. That way your efforts of, ah, holding up the sky would not go unnoticed."

"Well," the pillar coughed a little self-consciously. "When you put it like that I suppose it would be a little selfish of us not to talk, to help our brothers become recognised for their great work, of course. Not for myself, you understand?"

"Of course," I answered, happy that I was finally going to get some information about this place.

"Well, the simple truth of the matter is that we all built ourselves. We are self-made pillars, but you must understand, we were not always stone. Once, aeons ago we were a great forest of wood and leaf. After growing for more than a thousand years we found that we all had as much sunshine as we needed, and were as tall as we could ever be. Obviously there had to be some sort of greater purpose for us to be here, so all of us started to talk with each other in order to find out what this greater role might be.

"Yes, we carried the nests for birds and the shade for our forest, but there had to be a higher purpose, because we were the highest and greatest of living things. Over time we realised that, of all our attributes, the singular fact that we were extremely tall was probably the most significant. Our natural and most reasonable conclusion as to why this were so became clear. Obviously the divine purpose we were created for was to hold up the sky.

"Clearly the Gods of the wood had grown us for this purpose, and so we all undertook it with great enthusiasm, straining up our branches to hold up the great sky itself. After a few centuries of this, your whole body became aligned to the vertical, but the more of the load we took the heavier the sky became. We had never realised the enormous nature of the task, but we grew stronger, and harder, in order to carry out our divine task.

"We hardened our mind and our emotions and our body, and refined every part of ourselves to fulfil this one great purpose. Finally our hearts turned to stone, and we became the magnificent pillars that you see here today. It also helped that we were now fire proof, so we can now exist without fear. Do you understand now, child, the very great and important role we play, and how much we have suffered for your sake?"

What can you say to a pillar of stone that believes it holds up the sky? They were indeed magnificent creations, and who is to say that in some way they were not holding up the great blue? I certainly could not say with certainty about what it is that holds up the heavens, but I have been to other planets with no great trees, and in these places the sky just seems to stay there. I decided to ask, "I have no doubt of your great age and the effort you have gone to, mighty Pillar. It is truly an extraordinary tale, but what I cannot understand is how, in other places, far away places, the sky seems to hold itself up."

"That is a very easy thing to understand," the pillar retorted. "Everyone else is too lazy to assist and we must do all the hard work on our own. Now please let me continue with my important task, because I cannot rest until it is finished."

"That might take a very long time," I suggested.

"That is what time is for" came the apparently stock answer from the Pillar, apparently very proud of his wisdom. "No one ever did anything of worth until they invested time enough in its doing."

I must say that the nature of the Pillars seemed paradoxical, a sort of self-fulfilling prophecy. It appeared that the great creation was saying no more, and seemed to be entirely disinterested in who built the road. I shrugged and moved on down the cobblestones.

The Indoor Astronomer

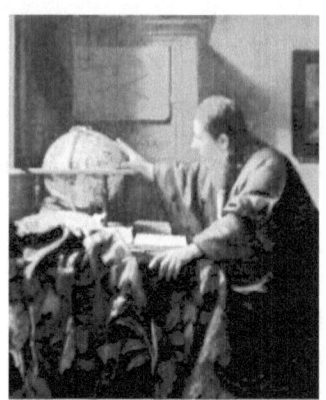

The great stone highway continued on for many miles, and finally I came across a cottage. Clearly someone was living in it, despite the derelict garden that surrounded it, because white smoke was coming from the chimney.

I knocked on the door. I was tired and would have liked a cup of tea, and this was the only house I had seen since leaving the village of the Ladder Men. Perhaps the local resident would be more talkative about things than the Pillars. There was no answer, so I knocked again, calling out "Halloooo! Is anyone home?"

"I am very busy" was the only response.

I found it difficult to image what would keep someone very busy out here in the wilderness, so I just waited for a moment and did nothing. A small deer stopped as it came out of a grove of trees, and looked at me before bundling off. Then I heard the door click, and with a slight squeak it opened to a tall, lanky fellow with long grey hair and a beard that almost reached his belly. He had a musty smell about him, like clothes left too long in a drawer.

He eyeballed me with his grey eyes, lifting his spectacles to get a better look, squinting, then putting them back down on his rather large, hooked nose. The face had that thin skin you see on old folk, but he seemed quite fit and sprightly. "Well. You want something? Yes?" he introduced himself with a question.

I was taken aback not by his brusque nature, but by the fact that behind him, though it was a bright day, I could see a hundred candles burning, and by their light I could see all sorts of large graphs and what seemed to be mathematical equations stuck up all over the walls. This was indeed a puzzle.

"Hello," I said. "I am travelling down this road, and I am not sure where it goes, and was looking for some advice." The man continued to stare at me, as if I had said nothing at all. So I added, "And I would really love a cup of tea!"

Suddenly his entire demeanour altered. The man smiled warmly, saying "Of course! You must be the fellow from the Astrological Association. Come in, come in, though I must warn you I do not hold a lot of stock in this prediction business. I look to the stars purely for their perfection and harmony."

With this I was ushered into what seemed the strangest world I had ever seen. Great charts were everywhere, with diagrams and arrows, and long lists of calculations, but most surprising of all, the whole ceiling was painted with what seemed to be a perfect representation of the night sky. I was going to explain that I was not from the Astrological Association, but then thought the better of it, as the man was quite happy, and was already pouring tea.

"It's so good to share tea with like-minded fellows, don't you think. Not like having to deal with the riff-raff and rubbish of the common man. No, we like educated talk, wisdom, philosophy and THINKING. All of the great books of the ages are OUR business, are they not? And without waiting for an answer, he continued.

"Yes indeed, it is a pleasure to have a noble soul like yourself sharing a few moments to contemplate the nature of the universe."

I still had said nothing, but already the fellow was bringing out large charts, and talking about the upcoming transit of Venus and asking me what this new fangled Astrology business made of this unique and rare circumstance.

All I knew was that Venus was the Planet of Love, so I said "Maybe love is coming into your world?" The man stared at me, as if in shock. Then he broke down briefly and wept, then apologised, then gathered himself and started talking about Jupiter.

This needed to be cut short, because he was looking as if he would be talking to himself (with me as his excuse) all day. So I simply asked exactly what I wanted to know. "Tell me friend, I have some questions about where you live. This is a very out-of-the way place, yet it has this perfect road. Who would have built such a thing, and do you know why?"

His demeanour changed completely. The man laughed, and shook his head. "You are an astute young man, aren't you? Yes indeed, that IS the real question is it not? Who DID make this road, and why? Who DID make these incredible maps that I have here, and why? The questions of the universe are always so deep and confounding, but we must never give up our search for them. Whoever it was that gave us THIS (he waved all about him) are sure to have hidden secrets of wisdom in these gems of truth, somewhere."

"The Jewel of Truth!" I said, finally finding a subject that I had some sort of connection with. "I had a dream about finding that!" but he cut me short.

"Ah yes, so do we all, do we not. A worthy dream, a great goal, a noble subject and one I am sure the architects of this great endeavour before us had asked, and more importantly, answered. If only we could uncover this message they gave us, what accolades it would herald, what a triumph it would be!"

I really could not continue with this, but I was curious, and asked "Why are you doing all of this?" I questioned, waving at all the charts.

"What? You don't believe I can achieve this end? You doubt me? Why I am shocked, dismayed, and distressed that you could be so forthright? After all, I have already discovered a great many things with my study! The elliptical orbit of Mars, for one thing. You tell me anyone who has described this! Anyone? I thought not."

"No, what I want to know is why do you stay inside this house with all these candles on during the day, when there is a world to be discovered at your doorstep."

The man scratched his nose with a long, slow motion. "I believe I see where you are coming from, Sir. The house is an analogy for my consciousness, and the world is the opportunity to expand. What you are suggesting is that I allow my imagination to run and not be concerned about the technical aspects of my work. Yes, I see. It makes sense. That's very insightful of you."

I was getting slightly exasperated. Nothing I said was simple to this man. "Let me put it another way. You have a universe of stars on your ceiling, yet if you enjoy the day and go outside at night, the universe will be there waiting for you. Do you look at the stars at night?"

"Do I look at the stars at night? Look at the stars?" he scratched his chin, pondering the conundrum. "I wonder what you mean. Oh, I get it!" the man held up a triumphing finger. "You are talking about the Dark Night of Soul, and how even in my deepest depression there is a universe to be discovered. Of course, it is so obvious. You are positively the wisest young man I have ever met. Here I am thinking my deep depression as a failing. The difficulty I have in unlocking the secrets of the ancients I truly believed was all my fault, but really, if I look through the depression I can see the stars are still here. The goal is still before me, regardless of the mood or the suffering I undertake.

"Here I was worrying about the eclipse of the moon being a day late with my calculations, and arriving on June 27th instead of the 26th as it should. Yet you are saying that the dark itself will resolve the question. Brilliant! Absolutely brilliant. Another cup of tea?"

"Ah, yes… Don't mind if I do," I said, baffled. Then I added, "This is the reason you look at your ceiling?"

"What? You are saying there is more to it? I have missed something? You hinted at outside looking at the stars, so therefore you are really saying that I need to get outside of MYSELF? I see, get away from my old patterns and start seeing things with fresh eyes. What does it matter if the next eclipse comes in 21 years, three months, 4 days, five hours and 17 minutes. It will all come as it does!

"Wonderful. Release thyself, dear Soul, and soar. All day and all night I have been looking at this ceiling, but you are saying let it all go! Let the imagination be free and see where it leads. And all this time I have been afraid of allowing it too much room, because it may have affected my beautiful, perfect calculations with useless dreams and nonsense, and I would be laughed at. But here you come, not laughing, and quite seriously saying this is the RIGHT thing to do.

"Release the creative imagination. Allow it to be free. Yes, wonderful. Well, thank you SO much for coming and sharing your wisdom with me. I will have much to think about and can only congratulate the Association for sending such a level-headed young man to speak to." And with this I was ushered out the door, where I was surprised by a young girl, who obviously was some sort of servant for the man.

She nodded politely to me, and so, before she went inside, I asked her about where the nearest town might be. "I have no idea Sir. I have never left these grounds. I tend the gardens, cook the food and do the washing for the Astronomer, and every week a delivery comes from the village of the Ladder Men with food and supplies. I suppose this is the closest village, but I saw you came from that way."

"Does the Astronomer always stay inside with all his charts and map of the heavens?" I asked.

"Yes Sir, he never leaves the house except to wash, which he does once a week."

"But at night, doesn't he look at the real stars, rather than the ones he has on his ceiling?"

"No Sir. He says that the atmosphere might cause them to disappear, or disturb things, and that the only stars that you can rely on are in his mathematics and the charts. I don't know why he does this, but this is what he does. I think he is my grandfather, but he never stops to talk, so I really don't know. He spends all his time reading books and studying."

"But what if the person who wrote the book is wrong about where a star is, surely you would think he might like to check things, just occasionally?"

"As I say Sir, I just don't know. I hope one day to know something, but my lot for now is here with the Astronomer, so I don't ask questions I know I can't answer. But he does say that if everything adds up, then everything is fine. Indeed, he worries constantly about everything adding up properly, so he adds and adds and adds things up all the time."

"Well, tell me. Do you think it is a good thing to try and work out the Universe from your books and your ceiling?" I asked, wondering if the girl thought about anything at all.

"Truly Sir, I do not live his life. It is not something I would like to do, but he is happy doing this, and he hurts no one. I am grateful that I have a place to stay, and though he is not a caring man for anything but his work, he is not unkind."

"So. you might want to leave when you get older? And if you do, where will you go?" It struck me as very odd that this young girl could be happy serving an old man who cared for nothing but books, but that maybe asking things this way she will give me a clue as to what it further down the road.

"Well, yes I would like to see the world, or at least more than this house. Perhaps in time. But unlike yourself I would not want to leave before I have somewhere to go. In the meantime, the full moon comes, the sunrises comes, small animals of the forest come to visit. Many things come to me here, just like you have!"

The simple truth the girl spoke struck me. She was wise because she knew she knew nothing, and was happy because she allowed life to give her what it would. She was almost the exact opposite of the Astronomer, who wanted to know everything and locked himself away from life.

I thanked her for the conversation, and started on my way down the road once more.

The Tavern

After this meeting I walked for a number of days before I found my next piece of civilization. By this time I was very hungry and tired, and the fruit by the road no longer sustained as it first did. I found myself wishing for a good hearty soup and a large chunk of bread to dip into it.

That was when I heard the noise and merriment rumbling up from a small dell, and down near the forest edge, off the road, there was a building, and behind that, many buildings. On its roof there was written in large letters the word "TAVERN" and in smaller letters underneath this, the word "FOOD and LODGING".

By the time I got close I could see that quite a large number of people were there. So far I had thought whole road almost deserted, for I had seen so little activity since the village of the Ladder Men. Yet here all was bustling and busy.

The cheery sounds of laughter and people enjoying themselves lifted my spirits. About me were thatched roofed houses, and a sense of business and bustle. Smiling faces of children playing games, old folk sitting by a small lake that was in the centre of the town, carpenters shops, candle shops, and all manner of trade.

I went into the tavern, and a large woman with a round red face who stood behind the bar asked me what I would like to drink. "Water" I said, for I realised I had no money for anything else. Well, she just laughed at this, and said they don't serve water, but if I am a horse there is a trough outside. I explained that I didn't have any money, but she just winked, put her fingers to her lips as if to say "don't tell anyone" and poured me a beer. I must say, it was wonderful after so many days camping out to sit amongst people and listen to their chatter.

Songs were in the air, and a piano was playing in the background. People were dancing, laughing and having a wonderful time, and I quite forgot all about the road, and the journey, or any question as to why I was here. There was so much fun and friendliness that I just didn't need to know anything else.

A woodsman came up to chat. He sat down and, after talking about the weather, he breathed a deep sigh, saying, "Wonderful here, isn't it? Life and all its problems simply wait outside, but inside we can play to our hearts content. I tell you, it was my lucky day, the day I found this place. I had been walking down the endless highway for God knows how long when I called in to have a drink, and I can tell you, the best decision I ever made. How about you, young fella? What brought you in?"

"Well, like yourself," I replied. "From where I had first met the Gardener there was this road that strangely called me to follow it. I had nowhere else to go, mind, but it seemed the right path to follow. Which is what I have been doing until a few moments ago."

The man oddly enough seemed to tense up. He gripped his glass as if he were fighting some invisible adversary. "SO, you too have met that damn Gardener, the one who put me through all my trouble."

I was at a complete loss for words. What can you say to something like this?

"Don't worry," the man continued, "I don't expect you to answer, there is no damn answer and that accursed road goes on forever. You do understand, don't you?" he peered at me intently, "That road has no end.

It just goes on and on. At least here we can stop, and be happy." And with this, the man broke down into tears.

I seemed to be finding a lot of men breaking down into tears. Then the bar woman came up, stoking the mans hair, "It's all right love. It gets to us all every now and then. It's not you (she said looking at me) but the way things are. It's just how life will treat us sometimes."

There was some softness to her voice that calmed me, made me feel warm and comfortable. Perhaps it was the beer I was unused to drinking, perhaps it was the atmosphere, but I started to feel some effect creeping over me. There seemed a sort of numbness. My mind stopped hearing things clearly, and a swirl of emotion and music and song came over me. Soon I found myself up there at the piano singing along to songs I didn't know with people I had never met, yet it all seemed to familiar, so friendly, and so easy.

Normally I would be curious and ask people where they came from, what they did, where they lived, but as the evening began to fall all I wanted to do was to laugh and sing and carouse. The sobbing man had recovered and he, too, was up and dancing the night away.

But I am very unused to all of this and after many hours had passed a great weariness came over me, and I wanted a bed to sleep in. But when I went to ask what I might do, I realised again that I had no money. Surely it was something I should have taken care of earlier, but I had been too busy enjoying myself. Shaking my head for my own foolishness, I remembered that there was a barn outside, and so I could probably find some straw and a place to curl up and sleep.

Staggering from the bar, because by now I was quite dizzy and disorientated, I made my way to the barn, only to find it locked. An owl called, "who whooo" and I looked in its direction. The moonlight seemed to show up a small glade, and finding my way there I saw a large tree trunk that had a hollow in it, so I crawled in and found a nice bed of twigs all laid out. I thought nothing of it, even though it must have belonged to someone, but I was so dizzy I passed out there and then.

It was night when I awoke to find myself being prodded. "Here here!" said a small angry voice. "Why do you think I made this bed, for other's to lie in it? I think not. Get up human, get up!"

I opened one eye to see a fox looking crossly at me. I am not sure why I said it, but I did without thinking, "But foxes have burrows, not nests of twigs in a tree trunk."

"Oh HO! A bright young spark we have here, don't we. Just testing to see if you are awake, but really, it's not your place and you really ought to get going." Said the fox, cocking his head to one side to see how I responded.

That was when it clicked, the fox had come in looking for an easy dinner, hoping to find whoever lived here fast asleep. But instead he found a human, who was far too big to eat. He just wanted me moved on so his dinner could come home. However, it is not every day you meet a talking fox, and he may know something about this road, so I asked him, "Do you know where this road leads?"

The fox was caught by surprise. "It leads many places. For me it leads to tasty chickens, for you it may lead to who knows what. Why are you worried about where it's going, and not about where you are?" Then his eyes narrowed, showing a little of his fox cunning.

"All roads lead to moments, and all moments lead to other things, but never away from the moment. And at this moment, I am quite hungry and you are spoiling my night." said the fox with some agitation.

"But aren't we all just another moment on the road?" I countered.

"Yes, maybe, but it's time to move to the next, so be off with you!" it commanded.

I was in no mood to be pushed about by a sly fox, and was still very tired, and I suspect very drunk. "You would have to tell me where the road led if you were to encourage me to get up and go there," I said, simply.

"All you will meet are stories. You go where the stories will lead you." said the fox.

Part of me wanted to chat, and to see if there was anything more to discover, the other part could see that the fox was quite tired himself.

"Are you far from your burrow?" I asked. I could see he was by the look in his eyes. "Why don't you curl up here, forget your hunger, and get some sleep. We can see what we see come the morning."

"You won't bite me, will you?" said the fox, looking a little timid all of a sudden.

I felt a great wave of kindness sweep over me. "Of course not," I said "I am too tired to be biting foxes tonight, so as long as you don't bite me, I think we will get on fine."

The foxes head hung heavy, and he seemed to say OK. He walked in, curled up with me, and soon after I passed back into dreams. And so it was, until morning broke to find me alone, but with a little fur on my shirt to remind me that it was not just a strange dream.

I got up and stretched, and in the distance I could still hear the Tavern and the songs. All night they had sung, and then I realised they were still singing the same songs, over and over. The cutting air of a brusque morning was like a tonic to my brain. I remembered the sobbing man, and his talk about the road going on forever, but what was the alternative? To go back to the tavern and sing the same songs over and over?

Somehow it was not so joyful to me now. I was hungry, so went up to the bakers shop in the village and asked if I could so some work in return for bread. He happily agreed, and I was cleaning pots and pans for a few hours, after which he equipped me with a good supply of day old bread, some oil, and some seasoning.

I left the village, sat down by a stream that was in the woods, and ate my breakfast. It felt wonderful. In fact, I felt so alive, out here in the woods with only myself and my thoughts that the Tavern started to look sad and uninviting. Would being here forever be such a bad thing? Was travelling the road, meeting many stories, as the fox pointed out: Was this not a good thing? Why did the sobbing man seem so desperate to be happy, yet so obviously unhappy?

I was not to know it, but soon I would meet someone who could answer that question. In the meantime, I looked at the road before me. No one in the village seemed to know much about it, for they rarely travelled far from their homes, and while the baker was happy for me to help, he said he did not seem to think it was a great idea to go travelling.

He, of course, wanted some help about his shop, and he said he would pay me enough for food and lodgings at the Tavern, but something told me that this was not a good thing to do. The call of the road was stronger than the need for comfort.

I thought then of my home, my little planet circling a far distant star. Then I thought of the Tavern, and by comparison it seemed a thin place. I am not certain how it could be so wonderful one night, yet by the next day it's joy could seem so faded, but it had. There was no turning back, I needed to follow the road until I found the way back home, or to wherever it might be that it led. This place was not my home, the people in the tavern were not really my friends. It was the open road that called, not the closed world of society.

The words of the Gardener came back to me at this moment, "We either move forward with love, or retreat from life with fear."

The Happy Sad Man

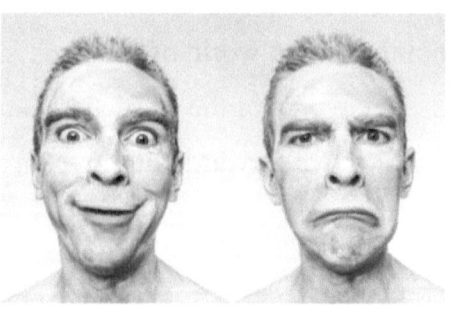

The road had gone from a state of natural wildness to cultivated fields, with wheat and vegetable crops in tilled rows, forming patterns against the landscape. As I made my way that day, I met someone who was possibly the most odd person of all.

The fellow was just standing by the side of the road as I walked along, and even at a distance I could see him acting quite strange. He would be rolling around on the ground in what I first thought was pain, but as I approached it seemed he was having an uncontrollable fit of laughter. Then, with no warning or apparent reason, he stopped and started sobbing uncontrollably. I stood there, watching, and soon he went back to hilarity, gripping his sides with humour, bordering on hysteria. Then he took up his sobbing once more.

This time, as he went back to laughter, I called over to him and asked what he found so funny. He didn't answer, only pointed his finger at me, and laughed all the harder. It is quite off putting to find oneself in the midst of some joke but not understanding it.

Then the laughter ceased, and he broke into fits of sobbing once more. I had come up quite close now. "What is it that makes you laugh one moment, then cry the next?" I asked. I was determined to get an answer, so stood there looking at him. At first he avoided my eyes, darting either side to avoid contact, but eventually he seemed to realise I was not going away, so he fixed his waterlogged eyes onto me.

He had an odd whine to his voice, like a beaten dog. His hair was dishevelled and his clothes were just rags, but his eyes (despite their misery) remained quite sharp. "It was so funny when you were walking up, but then I realised you were coming over, and I panicked, which caused me great suffering, then I realised how stupid this was because I had never met you, then I remembered all the people I had met but who I no longer saw, then I realised this proved the fact that at least I was still alive, then I realised you wanted to ask me questions, and I really do not deal with stress: And that's where I am at the moment. Satisfied? I am stressed."

And with this, he broke out once more into a maniacal laugh, and started dancing with glee kicking his knees up into the air. I thought he must simply be mad, and started to walk on, but he stopped me. He grabbed me and said quite ferociously, "I knew you wouldn't get the joke! No one EVER gets the joke."

"You didn't even tell me a joke." I retorted, slightly annoyed.

"LIAR!" he shouted. "Everything I have done and said since you first saw me told you about the joke. You are too stupid to get it, that's all."

"Look Sir, I didn't even realise you were telling me a joke. If I don't know you are putting some riddle to me, how can I understand what it might mean?" I waited for him to answer, but he had collapsed into fits of weeping once more. I prompted him back to the present "Er, did you hear it before I arrived?"

Life sprung back into him like a bolt of lightning. "You didn't hear the joke? I can't believe it! How could you have not heard the JOKE? Everyone knows the JOKE!" He hung there in space, like a jack in the box that had popped.

"I am very sorry Sir, but I most definitely have not heard the joke. Perhaps if you told it to me, I would understand?"

"You don't understand, do you? The joke is not something you say, it isn't even really something you do. It is something that IS. Do you see? It's right in front of your nose, but you can't see it, and THAT's funny. But it is also terribly sad. Everyone here knows the Joke, and everyone is laughing about it."

I must say, the fellow was exasperating. He had such intensity in everything he did and said, but it seemed to all be to no purpose. "I really wish I could see what was so funny," I said, "But I simply do not. Perhaps I had better be going."

He burst into sobbing once more, saying "No don't go! I am so lonely. I am all alone here, with my joke that you don't understand, which makes me happy, but I know you don't like me, which makes me sad, and I don't know what to do about it, which makes me miserable, yet I hope that if you stay." He suddenly started brightening up, and went back to his happy face. " If you STAY, then everything will be fine and dandy. You will get the joke soon enough, I am sure you will."

I did feel for this strange man, so I put my hand on his shoulder and asked "Why don't you just tell me what the joke is? Then perhaps I will understand?"

He burst into sobbing once more, and I was at quite a loss as to what to do next. "The JOKE! The JOKE!" He said with eyes full of pain. "Everyone gets the joke, everyone laughs at it. Everyone thinks how ridiculous it is, and they point and laugh whenever it passes. No one knows how much pain the joke suffers, or how the ridicule bites, or what pointlessness everything has."

Finally I understood. The Joke was HIM.

I held him by the roadside for quite some time and eventually he managed to calm down. Finally he seemed to sober up, and looked up at me without either the mad laughter or the overt misery in his eyes. "You asked me why I laughed? It is very simple, really. When I am laughing I am not crying, and the world is wonderful!"

He started to dance another jig on the roadside, and he sang an odd melody as he did so"

"I laugh when I don't cry
   It's an easy thing to try
   You laugh and laugh
   Until you sigh
   Then you cry and cry and cry
   I don't know why"

And with this song, he began to weep once more, and then ran away into one of the neighbouring fields. At first I had thought to call him the "Happy Sad Man" but as I thought about it, he was really just a very sad man. A very, very sad man.

The Yes No Man

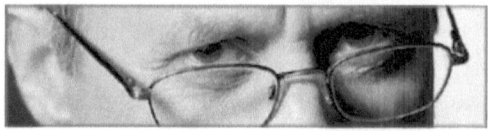

Soon after the chance meeting with the Happy Sad Man, another odd character turned up. A fellow came up on me from behind, and caught me completely by surprise. It was not just his sudden appearance, but mostly I was shocked by the gruff, demanding tone of his voice.

"Well! Are you doing something useful, or not? Yes or No!" he demanded. Even though it was supposed to be a question, it was clear he was not interested in an answer. It also appeared that this was as good as you got from him by way of introduction.

"People. Aimlessly wandering along, no purpose at all. No goal, no direction, and they wonder why they don't get anywhere. It's because they are not GOING anywhere, that's why there is the problem." This rude man wore a striped 3 piece suit with a bowler hat, and black patent leather shoes. He had a black umbrella over his left arm, a briefcase in his right hand, and a very severe attitude that was emphasised by one raised, arched eyebrow.

"Well, what is your answer? No point beating about the bush, boy. Too many people willy-nilly about and then they have the gall to complain that nothing gets done!" He paused for a moment, obviously waiting for me to answer his demands, but I really had no idea what he wanted to know.

"Perhaps you weren't listening?" he continued. "I asked a very simple question and I expect an answer. Are you doing something useful, or not?"

"Well, that depends." I went to answer but he cut me short.

"Depends on what? How long it takes for you to concoct up some fairy tale for yourself? You are either doing something useful, or you are NOT!" He finished with a clipped voice of absolute certainty.

"NO" I answered firmly, "It depends on whether what I think is useful is the same as what you think is useful."

"Codswallop and hogwash. Useful things have value," he snapped back. "Show me something has value and I will see that it is useful. It is very simple, very clear, now what is your answer?"

"My answer is that I find a sunrise very useful, because it lightens my day. I find the wind in my face useful because it cools me." I thought I was being defiant, but in truth it was water off the ducks back to the thick skinned this fellow.

"Bah! You are making excuses because you don't want to admit that you are useless. Admit it, you are not doing anything useful, are you? The facts are clear, everyone gets a sunrise every day. This does not make the sunrise useful as far as YOU are concerned. It is obvious the sun is being useful, because it allows us to be productive by giving us light. But that's the SUN being useful! You are not useful, are you?"

"That's an accusation, not a question." I protested.

"Caught out are we? Caught out wandering about being completely useless? A good-for-nothing wastrel wasting the very air that they breath. A no-hoper simply occupying space and idling away their time."

I didn't know what to say. It was a standoff, and I was finding myself quite unwilling to have anything more to do with this man. Yet I could not quite walk away. I had a sense that there was something more to all of this. Then a thought occurred to me.

"I tell you want, I have a question for you, and if you answer it properly it will answer your first question to me. Do you want to try it?"

I offered. I suspect his curiosity got the better of him, because he stood in deep thought for quite some moments, wondering what he might be getting himself into.

"What sort of question, and why should I answer it?" he probed with a reasoning caution.

"It's a very simple question, and you do not have to answer it if you don't want to. After all, it is something that you may wish to go away and think about."

He looked at me suspiciously, but finally relented. "Very well, ask your question. But I do not promise to answer it."

I smiled, because I had the perfect question, "Why do you ask ME if I do something useful or not?"

"Why that's an easy one. There are far too many people wandering about doing nothing useful, but who fool themselves into believing the opposite. They need a firm hand to point them on their way, so they stop wasting time and become productive members of society."

Finally the fog of confusion lifted from my mind. "Oh, I see! This is how YOU do something useful, isn't it?"

"Yes, of course. That is obvious, and should have been obvious from the start. But you now have to answer my first question, yes? I don't see how my answer answers your lack of being useful, not at all."

"It is answered, though you don't see it yet. We are both on the road to find out. This is our shared purpose, and it makes us brothers." I must say, this is the first time I ever realised the simplicity of my journey. I really was on the Road to Find Out.

"Find out what?" he demanded, not convinced at all.

"How to walk more closely with the heart" I answered.

This seemed to stop him completely. I heard no words from him as he thought about this notion from what must have been a hundred angles in his mind. I must say, he seemed less gruff and as I waited for him to speak, more and more I saw an honest soul genuinely seeking to make a positive difference to the world.

"I see," he said at last, in a fairly categorical sort of voice. "You have a goal and your purpose on this road is defined. This is good. As long as you are not being a burden on anyone, of course?" He queried with that raised eyebrow again.

"Oh, I am looking after myself, all right." I assured him.

"Well then my work has not been in vain. Being closer to the heart is the heart of true purpose, and a pleasure to meet someone else who has realised this. A man who loves his work loves his life, and anyone who loves life cares for it. I wish you well on your endeavours young man," and with this he abruptly turned about, went up to a nearby rock, and asked it "Well? Are you doing something useful, or not?"

Back at the campfire, he trailed off as he finished his last tale. The night had slipped past unnoticed, and in the enchantment of his many stories we both fell into the world of dreams. We just gazed at the fire for quite some time in silence. I don't even recall falling asleep, but as the images of his journey twirled and danced in my thoughts, everything else was forgotten.

What amazed me was how it was all so real to him. That the next day I wanted to know more.

Intermission

Little was said that following morning. Perhaps he was all talked out, and I felt it right not to ask for more. He would talk in his own time. He spent a good part of the morning holding some of the crystals and rocks I had found up to the sunlight, and just gazing into whatever he found there.

I simply did camp chores. Gathering firewood, cleaning cooking pots, bringing in fresh water, and preparing a breakfast he barely noticed, but ate anyway.

The day was well into the afternoon by now. I got some late lunch prepared and gathered a few more sticks for the fire. He just sat there, gazing away into space, lost in some other world.

I said little, but as I worked I realised something quite extraordinary. In all the stories he had been telling me, there was the silhouette of a hundred people I had met. In truth, I could place the faces of many people I saw in my everyday life over the descriptions the child was giving in his stories. My drunk co-worker who preferred the tavern to his life, the boss who was always driving us to be productive. The professor who worked in accounts, he was like the man who never got his head out of his books.

The Pillars were like those rigid men who stood at the parish church when I was growing up, looking and sounding important. We have a few of those at work as well. And as this thought came to me, I realised that I was the Happy-Sad Man. Sad at work, happy when leaving. It was a very two-faced existence. This is what really made me want to leave the place.

I dawdled with my thoughts till the evening began to fall. The child was still with me, and had found some wild mushrooms and fruit from somewhere nearby. Fried mushroom on buttered toast, with fruit slices! It was something you might get in an expensive restaurant, and out here in the woods the odd combination was a delight. It felt a little strange, sitting there eating this fine food as we sat under the growing light of the moon, mere nobodies. A repast fit for a king being eaten by peasants. It tickled my sense of irony.

The moon had risen now, come full up over the horizon, and leaving a bright candle of light shimmering on the lake. A soft breeze picked up, and swayed its reflection like a belly dancer, and for no reason we laughed. All my troubles had fallen away and I felt free as a bird.

Partly this was because I had managed to stop interrupting his stories with questions. All my life I had been too curious for most people, always asking what they meant when they said this or that. But with this child the pleasure of his stories were like a wave you rode. I simply didn't want to bump into things with unnecessary questions, and what a great pleasure this was.

Now for you, who takes life as it comes, this may not seem like any great matter at all, but for serious little me, just doing nothing but paying attention was a wonderful, releasing experience. I was like a great ship rolling down a wide river, enjoying the view. I had little need for anything but more stories.

I recalled when he met the ladder men, that he mentioned how he had given up everything for his freedom, and yet it was free, despite it's cost. I had never really thought about it till now. Of course, as a child you were free, despite any orders you had to follow. So why didn't I feel the same way at work?

More and more I was coming to realise that the problem with my workplace was myself. Perhaps I had judged others too harshly? I mean, we had salesmen, and they were always selling themselves. It had annoyed me, but now I see that this is just how they are. And the Ladder Men? Who would they be? It would have to be the marketing crew, always building things up, and making them sound far more important than they really are.

The child's story was also mine, in this sense. But isn't this true of all good stories?

Later that evening after we had had supper, and when chatted about nothing in particular, the boy continued with his tale. He seemed less distant now, and as he spoke he often looked at me directly, rather than off into the distance.

He started with a laugh, saying "Perhaps the Astrologer could have been tempted to come out to see the stars if I told him they were hiding here in this lake!"

"All you would have to do was bring him here," I suggested "And perhaps he would not want to stay indoors so much." I added, but this made the boy grow serious again.

"No" he said, "First the man would have to WANT to come here, and that first step is the hardest of all steps to take." Then, gathering his thoughts, he continued with his tale.

The Incredibly Un-Helpful Helpful Man

After meeting the odd fellow who wanted to know whether everyone (including rocks) were doing something useful, or not, I then came up to a road side stand that said, "Free Fruit Juice". Well, that was just what I needed, so I went on up to ask for some.

An extraordinarily enthusiastic fellow came forward, and introduced himself, "Dashing! Jacob Dashing at your service Sir. What may I do for you today?"

He seemed very professional, and was dressed in a clean, white shirt, tie and jacket. with blue pants and white leather shoes. He had bright red hair, blue eyes, and an extremely eager attitude. It seemed that all he wanted to do was to please me in some way. "Well," I answered, "I would like a fruit juice, please."

"A wise choice, if I may say so myself, and one that will be completed to your greatest satisfaction within mere minutes. I assure you, there will be only joy and pleasure that you will experience here, at this stand. Now, if you could let me know what you would like, I will get right to it!"

I looked at him with a slightly puzzled expression, "I, er, already ordered a fruit juice. You know, the one that you are offering free?"

"A wise selection and indeed you are correct. This free fruit juice is indeed exactly this, free. This is to say there will be no charge what-so-ever for the fruit juice. However, we must first answer an important question: Would you like this in a paper cup, or a glass?"

"Well, I would like a glass. But is this free as well?" I answered, suspecting that this might be the trick behind the so-called free juice.

"Extremely intelligent choice, if I must say so, and I do! A wonderful choice and I prefer the glass myself, every single time. And what would it be that you would like in that glass, Sir?"

"Ah … well… Fruit juice?"

"Brilliant! And did you know we are providing fresh fruit juice FREE today?"

It seemed to be going in circles. "Well, this is what your sign said" I answered, trying to remain polite.

"Oh ho! So you read the sign, hey? Well that's absolutely marvellous. It proves definitively that our advertising works. No question about that, is there?"

"If there's no question about it, why are you making it a question?" I asked.

"Mais Non! C'est la question pour la Monde. N'est ce pas?" He said, waving his hand apparently at what was around him. I paused, somewhat dumbfounded as to where this was all going. "Do you speak French?" he then asked.

"Well not really."

"The question you asked is really a question for the whole world, Sir. Advertising is the medium of communication for all cultures, all worlds, all people and even alien life forms. It's an incredible thing because it makes things HAPPEN. Why you are here because of ADVERTISING! This is self-evident. You know it, I know it, the whole world knows it. So, why are we asking questions about it? Let's just accept it as it is, and get on with it."

By now I had grasped the notion that this was an extremely odd person before me. He had complete and total enthusiasm for every single thing that came through his head, but he didn't seem to remember what the thing was he had enthusiasm for just two moments ago. "Free juice?" I prompted.

"Exactly… Exactement! Perfect! This is the key note of the advertising, thus you have proved its effectiveness. Thank you so much. I sweated over that sign for days, trying to get the wording just right, and here you are, which proves the effort was worthwhile."

"In a glass." I prompted again.

"Much better than a paper cup, I wholeheartedly agree. A wise choice, indeed, the best possible choice. No question, is there?"

"But if there is no question, why did you keep insisting on making everything a question?" I asked, quite amazed at the long and circular path this effort to get a free fruit juice was taking.

"WHY is there no question about the glass being better? The economical benefits of glass far outweigh paper in the long term, and there are no trees cut down as well. What is more, all you do is clean it and it is ready for use again and again, and again. Furthermore you are not constrained as to what you put into your glass. Why you could even put empty glasses in your glass. (he laughed at his apparently funny joke) It a wonderful, fabulous and extraordinary thing, don't you agree?"

The really remarkable thing was, for the ENTIRE time he had talked he had somehow managed to retain a broad smile. I am not sure that he even managed to breath in, but if he did, he smiled while doing it. I was fearing that the free fruit juice was going to cost me a lot of time, so I cut to the chase. "I would like my free fruit juice in a glass, now, if I may."

"Certainly Sir. Right away." And with this the fellow ducked down and disappeared behind the counter. He popped up on the other side of a rock that was off to my right. "Just a minute Sir. Won't be long!" and he appeared again to my left from behind a tree. "Just a few minutes more!"

Finally he appeared up from behind the counter with a paper cup in his hand, and giving it to me he said "Have a wonderful day!"

Well, I had been enjoying a wonderful day, up to this point. I looked into the paper cup, and it was empty. "Ah, this is a paper cup, and there is no fruit juice in it." I suggested.

"Quite correct Sir. Due to the incredible success of our advertising we have completely run out of our stock of glasses, and as a result, also our total supply of fruit juice. However, if you take this cup it will act as coupon to ensure that the next time you are visiting up that you will be provided with free fruit juice. That will be five dollars, thank you."

"Five dollars?" I said, amazed. "What for?"

"It's for the coupon, which is that cup you hold, and to help defray advertising expenses," Jacob Dashing said, and I must admire him for he managed to do so with a completely straight (yet smiling) face.

I placed the empty cup on his counter, saying "Perhaps I will skip the free fruit juice offer after all."

"A very wise choice, given the circumstances, Sir. And may I say what a great pleasure it has been to serve you today!" He continued smiling and waving to me as I left him, and started back on the journey down the road. Out of curiosity I looked back before I went around the bend that would put me out of his sight, and there he was: Still smiling, still waving.

I had no idea what this man was about, or what purpose he served, if any. Yet the entire time he never wavered in his enthusiasm for whatever it was that he imagined his purpose might have been. This seemed the oddest of the odd I had met so far, for the fellow seemed genuinely oblivious to the obvious.

What WAS certain was that his enthusiasm did not match his ability.

A Well Connected Man

This next man appeared quite normal, that is, normal if you though someone sitting at a desk in an open field with only a cardboard cut out of office walls around him, was normal. He was dressed as would any businessman, short hair, well trimmed nails, clean hands, crisp, starched white shirt, well ironed dark pants with a matching coat hanging over his chair, and a very simple, business tie.

There were no unwelcome creases in his clothes, but there was one quite severe one between his eyebrows, one that spoke of a very deeply considered man. He had bushy eyebrows, which betrayed a certain degree of wildness, but apart from that there was nothing in his external appearance to presume that he was anything but the respectable man going about his business. Except for the fact that the desk he sat behind was completely covered in telephones, and behind this was a table that was awash with cakes and pastries, and there were three chefs off to the side, in a field kitchen who seemed busy preparing yet more baked goods, presumably for the man.

As I stood and watched I saw the fellow go through a very conspicuous routine of self-importance. He would pick up a phone, make a call, speak for a few minutes, then hang up. After hanging up he preened himself in a hand mirror, checking his hair and clothes, as if to confirm that all his attire was in order. Then he made another call on another telephone, and repeated the process.

Then, on every third call, he would hang his head in abject misery, burst into tears like a little baby, and turn about and eat a fist full of pastries and sweets. He would shovel these into his mouth, snorting like a pig, then he would grab his stomach and throw up into a bucket. He did this at least five times before I interrupted.

"Excuse me Sir, but may I ask why you do this?"

"Do what?" he demanded, looking up at me with bloodshot eyes. "Why do I do WHAT?" he said with a striking vehemence. This quite caught me by surprise, because he hardly looked a violent soul.

There seemed no reason for his sudden anger, nether-the-less I apologised if I upset him, yet I really wanted to know what he was doing. "I do not mean to intrude, but why do you sit here, making all those calls, then burst into tears, and then eat all those pastries before throwing up into a bucket?"

"What's wrong with that?" the man said. "I can do it if I want to. It's my life, isn't it?" He drew himself up into a regal position, wiped away any vestige of tears with a red handkerchief that he found in his top pocket, and then questioned me. "Why do you ask, anyway? I can't see that it is any of your business what I, or anyone else, does, yes?"

"Well, it does seem, different, shall we say. After all, most people have only one telephone on their desk, yet you have at least 30. And while I agree, what you do is completely your business, I am just an interested Soul walking this road. I meet many people, and I am always wanting to understand them."

The man looked at me cautiously. Lifting his nose as if his nostrils were taking aim, he said "Very well then, I shall explain it to you." (He had a definite air of nobility about him as he spoke, I must say)

"I am a person of extremely high social standing. I am respectable and respected. By all social mores, codes and standings I am considered impeccable in both behaviour, fashion sense, and cleverness of wit. I have many friends, all of whom I contact by telephone, which is, of course, a mutually agreed thing in-as-much as should my friends wish to contact me, they will do so by telephone as well.

"Naturally I have many telephones because if any of my friends call me when I am on the line to someone, then I can answer them and assure them I am not being rude by ignoring their kindness. Should they call to find my line engaged, it may well cause them offence. Therefore it is a courtesy to my friends that I have over 30 telephones."

"But," I hesitantly suggested, "Surely you can only speak to one person at a time?"

"My dear impertinent child" he responded, "I can take a message and call them back. It is so much more personal than a mere message service, and of course, it is all along the accepted lines and procedures, and therefore quite above criticism.

"In fact, the simple self-evident truth that I have 30 telephones proves to all and sundry that I am indeed a very well connected man."

What can anyone say to this? It seems mad, but this is how his world worked. "Well, then why do you cry every third telephone call?" I asked.

The man's demure regard cracked with this question. Once more he broke down into uncontrollable tears (Why do so many people cry so much on this road?) and instinctively he reached over for a fist full of pastries, and stuffed them into his mouth. Finally, as the binge ended he looked up, seemingly disappointed that I was still here, and grudgingly he muttered underneath his breath some words about "deathly boring"

"Pardon me," I said "I didn't quite catch that?"

He angrily spat out his explanation, "Because those miserable toads I talk to are so damn boring. They are the dullest, most pig-headed, innocuous, frivolous and useless batch of nere-do-wells you could ever have the misfortune to meet. That is why I cry, because that is my lot in life, to be part of their small and pathetic world of nothing. That's why I cry, because all my friends are idiots, and that's why I eat, to try and make myself happy again."

"But you have 30 telephones," I protested. "You could just call up new people, more interesting folk, and make your life more interesting."

The man looked horrified at this suggestion. "I couldn't do that," he protested.

"Why not" I asked.

"Because I don't have anyone else's number, and it would be very rude to call someone if they have not formally given you their number."

"But surely you go out and meet new people? Surely they might give you a new number to call then?"

"No, I never go out. None of my friends ever have a party, so I never get invited to any. So I am stuck with the people I know."

"Well at least the cakes cheer you up, just a little."

"No" he cried, "They only make everything worse because they remind me how deathly bored I am.

"Oh dear," I answered, "You really have a significant and awkward problem here. Is there no way around it at all?"

"None," he answered. "I have thought about this for a very long time, and there simply is no way out of it. It's quite a trap, really."

"You could just walk away?" I suggested.

"And where would I go?" he responded, gloomily. "No, there is simply no solution other than bearing the load as best I can. I live in hope that one of my boring friends will one day meet someone interesting, and share my number with them. You never know!"

"Well that's true" I said. "We never know what is around the next corner, do we? "Well, I wish you the very best, and hope that you find a solution to all of this one day." But as I went to leave, he called me back.

"Wait! You must give me your number before you go!"

"I don't have a telephone," I answered.

"Well then, take MY number, and call me anytime you need to have a chat about anything." The man said, seeming rather hopeful that this might brighten up his life.

"I will take down your number, and I do promise that, if I am every back in this area, and if I find a telephone, that I will give you a call."

"Thank you," he said with a small tear in his eye, "Thank you very much."

"You could come with me down the road for a bit, and see if we meet anyone interesting?" I suggested.

"Oh I couldn't do that." he answered. "What if the telephone rang?"

Indeed, it was quite a predicament for him.

The Apple Cart Man

As I walked along, pondering the man with all the telephones, I began to think about how anyone makes a new friend, because this is all he really needed. Yet the more I thought of it, the more I realised he wasn't the sort of person I would be comfortable with as a friend. This got me to thinking about my Rose. Surely I loved her, but was it mutual?

The words of the Gardener came back to me: "She may not have legs, but she has a heart, and when this moves on in any friendship, the part that was cherished fades, and it appears that your flower dies"

He looked right at me, saying, "Perhaps I was no more to her than the man with the telephones was to me? It was not a pleasant thought, yet perhaps this is only unpleasant because it was true. I had no answer, and could not know because she was no longer here to ask. And even if she were, she may well lie, because she had a frailty in this regard."

Then I became distracted by yet another man on the road ahead, who seemed to be very preoccupied keeping a two-wheel horse cart balanced. I thought he was rehearsing some circus act, because as I got closer he seemed to be practicing a clown routine. He would steady the cart, balancing it precariously on its two wheels, then jot something down in his book. Then something would fall off and he would have to catch it, but this upset the cart, so he had to steady it again.

As I got closer I saw him repeat the routine many times, and then I realised it was a cart full of apples. "What are you doing?" I called out to him as I approached.

"No time!" he called back, "No time to answer. I have far too many things on my mind and as you can see I am very preoccupied and have more than enough to deal with as it is."

And he repeated the routine one more time, just for me. He balanced the cart, went to writing something down in his notebook, then an apple would roll off, which meant he dived to catch it. But the falling apple upset the cart, so he had to put it back in the best spot and look to balance the whole thing again.

I applauded his fine act, but he seemed to pay little attention apart from a single askance look that appeared to say "What? Are you still here?" as he frantically made more notes in his book. I gathered he would have preferred me to move on, but I was curious. Perhaps he needed help, or perhaps he was rehearsing for the circus.

"Do you need any help?" I asked.

"Don't upset the apple cart!" he said, loudly. And with this he continued his efforts, but it seemed to me that it was a losing battle, and the odd apple was getting away. He was a young man, perhaps 20, and very intense looking. It seemed pointless, and yet at the same time appeared to be very important, for some reason I could not fathom.

"Are you training for the circus, then?"

"Are you totally blind." he exclaimed. "Off course this is no circus act, though metaphorically speaking one might say that all our actions are demonstratively part of a universal Circus of sorts. No, I must keep the apple cart balanced, and I must finish my writing. It's a tiresome and difficult task I have been given."

I tried a different tack. "What are you writing about?" I asked.

"Oh, important stuff. Wonderful important stuff. But I have barely any time to write at all, because I have to keep balancing this cart. I am cursed and afflicted with this terrible task, but I must not complain for it is my duty." He trailed off to a sort of muttering.

"I think I can help you balance your cart, which will allow you more time for writing," I said, trying to keep things simple.

The fellow stopped, his jaw open. "But how? I have been trying for days, and I cannot get it balanced."

I picked up a stout branch from the ground, broke it off at the right height, and propped it under the front of the cart. "You see, now it has a third point of contact, and it is stable. As long as you don't bump it, you can write without interruption."

He went back to try and check if the cart was balanced, and he purposely bumped it unsteady again. But I caught it, and propped the branch back under the front draw-bar, saying "There's no need to touch it. Leave it, and it will stay there."

This time he paid attention, and stood back to see what would happen. To his amazement, the cart stayed up. "Remarkable." He said, impressed. "That is really a brilliant notion you had there. And to think, all this time I was so concerned about upsetting the apple cart."

Whereupon the young man proceeded to completely ignored me, and buried his head in his writing, never speaking another word. I am sure it was not that he was ungrateful, and only that he was long overdue on the task his heart desired, but it did seem a little rude of him.

I must admit, a part of me wanted to kick out the stay, and watch him frantically try to collect all the apples as they ran all over the road. Of course, I didn't. I didn't even stop to ask him what he was writing about.

I felt sad, but then I remembered what the Riddle Turtle had said "If it's not obvious, it's not worth it." And I got a different look at this apple cart business. Because the obvious was not able to be seen by the man, when I showed it to him he didn't appreciate it. But if he had discovered it himself, he would have felt great satisfaction and joy. So in a sense, by solving his problem I took away his freedom to find out for himself.

The obvious was worth little to him because he hadn't seen it. It was worth a lot to me because I had. I cannot expect him to value something that I made valueless for him, so it was my fault that he was ungrateful.

He looked up again at me with those sea green eyes, as if looking for my thoughts on the subject. I had to stop and gather them, because I was more in his story than my own thoughts. All I could think of was all the times I had helped someone out, and had barely received a nod of thanks. Perhaps he was right.

I was quite tongue tied, but if he were correct, then everything I was taught when growing up was wrong. "Are you saying we cannot help others?" I asked.

"No," he answered, 'We can try to help others, but are we stealing their chance to solve their own puzzle? It's like you with your crossword. What if it came out already finished? What fun would it be then?"

I had to agree, but I must say it still felt like something was missing. "But the Gardener helped you, didn't he?"

"Yes, but only because he let me help myself. I don't have the answer to why my rose went missing, but I am starting to understand that my love for her planted a seed inside my heart, and I can feel it growing.

"This sense of something growing, of something around the corner seemed to be getting stronger. And that was when I met the woodworker."

The Woodworker

He had a fine workshop filled with many large and powerful tools of trade. The smell of sawdust reached down the road, and it was this that first attracted me. He was hard at work, chiseling at some furniture and didn't notice me, so I sat quietly and watched him craft out a chair leg from what seemed and old limb from a tree.

What had been useless he made useful, just by his efforts. Beside him I saw other legs and pieces that had been similarly carved, and as I watched he started putting it all together in a most ingenious fashion. Just by using lengths of string and rope, he tied all the pieces into place, and then using a soft hammer, he tapped everything until it all locked up.

Then drilling a few holes for dowels, he shimmied these into place, set the chair to rights on the ground, and stepped back, smiling with his result. "110%" was all he said before he picked up some another apparently useless piece of wood, and started to carve it to the shape he desired.

Perhaps it was hours I watched, but after a time he stopped his work, and seeing me he smiled and waved me over. "I am just about to make tea. Would you like some?"

"Yes please," I answered. Quite honestly, I was happy to meet someone who seemed normal. As we went into the inside of his workshop, I noted many fine chairs and tables and kitchens and all sorts of woodwork displayed. "Is all of this work your creation?" I asked.

"Every bit of it, and everything 110%," he answered.

"110% ? I don't quite understand."

"Everything I do, everything I make, everything that leaves my shop must contain more than my best effort, it must contain my love. I love taking useless things, the wood no one believes to have any worth, and reworking it so that it becomes a thing of beauty. The bend in the bough that made it useless to the carpenter becomes the graceful movement of an arm in a chair, and so I turn the very thing that made the timber unwanted and useless into a thing of beauty.

"This is the surprise I have every day, that some odd thing works and becomes more than it is. And when I put it all together with other useless bits, it all becomes more than the sum of its parts."

I remembered what the Gardener had told me at the start of this journey, and I must have spoken it out loud. *"Every big thing is made from lots of little things. It is what every big thing must always remember, and what every little thing must never forget."*

"Yes!" said the woodworker, "That is exactly it. The things we believe are useless and not worth the effort, well with a little work, and a little love, and a little belief , we can transform them to make something much larger than those small useless bits could have ever imagined. But it takes 110%. It takes all your best effort, all your love, and all your focus to make it happen."

That was when I realised something very simple, which is that everything can be made useful when grasped by the master's hand.

As he poured me some tea, he breathed in the smell of the wood. "I love this place. I love my work. I love my life." He said. "I am the luckiest man in the world, because I have found true contentment. So little one, tell me what brings you to this place in the deep wood?"

Like yourself, I told him the outline of my story. The Salesman, the Gardener, the Long Road, and then I asked him if he knew the people who made this road in the first place.

"Perhaps I do. Not that I know the builders, for they are in the far past, but I can know them by their work." And with this he motioned me outside. "You see these paving stones? (I nodded) Well, see how closely they interlock. This is not to look pretty, but to stop water seeping in. And you see how the road has this arch shape, ever so small, but there? (I nodded again) This is to help the water move off the road when it rains. And you see how the whole road takes that line through the wood, never moving up or down, but staying flat? (I nod) Well, this shows me that a great deal of forethought, care, love and attention went into the building of this road.

"This is how I build furniture, so I know how these men thought. And they thought '110%'. Now as to WHY they build this road, I don't ask that question. Why do I build furniture? Because it is a beautiful thing to do. There is no other reason, and someone will find it useful. I love creating, and so did they. When we see something that is clearly build with love, and a passion for excellence, we can know that there is far more to it than the sum of its parts.

"And if we look too hard at the parts, we risk losing the whole.

"I love this place, and in my heart I know it loves me. The forest gives me everything I need to make a living and I return the favour by sharing its gifts with the world. We are one, the forest and I, just as my furniture and I are one. Separate, yet one, all the same." He closed his eyes, and just smelled the air, and sighed.

"Do you know where the road leads?" I asked, wondering if he had found the end.

"It leads me here," he said, simply. "That's all I need to know. But here is a special place, because at the end of my day, at the end of my thoughts, at the end of my feelings, right here is where I stay. It's my heart, my oasis and my friend."

With this he got up to go back to work, He didn't seem to mind me being there, so I made myself useful and went out collecting what I thought may have been workable pieces from the trees and branches that had fallen to the ground in the forest surrounding his workshop.

I was there for many days, and we talked about many things. I can truly say that here was someone who had found their place, as had the Gardener. He had the same loving devotion to every aspect of his business, and the same kind attention to the details.

He told me many stories of people who had stumbled onto this place, people who had come from far distant worlds looking for something, just like I had. Finally, after some days he asked me, "And do you know why you are here?"

I had to admit that I did not. The woodworker just smiled. "Can you see that every person you met has planted a seed in your heart? You offered them a seed, a part of yourself that wanted to help, but were they able to accept it? I think not. Yet you were able to accept what they had to offer. I suspect this may be why you are here: To learn acceptance."

The thought rang true. I had always thought the purpose of my journey was a destination to be discovered, somewhere in the far distance, but perhaps the experience of it was all there was to know.

I loved my time with the woodworker, and would have stayed there for longer except that one day when I was out gathering wood I came to the end of the road, which was just on the other side of this lake.

The Arrival at the Beginning

T he road ends here?" I asked, amazed because I had seen no road. "This is how you came to be here in the woods?"

"Yes," said the child, wistfully. "It would seem that as I arrived at a place of contentment, I came to the end of the road. But in truth, I am not content. I am happy enough, but I still miss my rose.

"And after all the travels down on that long road, I am still no closer to home. A single tear formed a rainbow that took me far away and despite all my travels and questions and experiences, I am no closer to what it is I seek. I don't even know what I am seeking. Maybe I should have just accepted the jewel the Salesman offered, even though I have no money."

From out the blue a loud, abrasive voice could be heard. "Listen kid, I told you that money is no problem. We got terms, we got deals, we got whatever you want. How many times have I got to tell you before you believe it?"

I twirled around, feeling like Alice tripping into Wonderland. There stood the most incredibly dressed man I had ever seen. He had bright plaid yellow pants, with an equally bright yellow jacket and under it, a striking red satin shirt with gold pins at the collar. Pink boots, red socks and the most extraordinary hat imaginable, made up of felt and fur and purple velour, struck with blue feathers that ballooned upwards.

"Ah, Jewels! Jewels indeed. Just what the doctor ordered. Here it is, one three carat beauty AND tell you what I will do: give me your decision right now and you get a 20% discount. Now, do we have a deal, or do we have a deal?"

The child sighed. "Sir," he said the salesman, "I do not have the money, I do not want the credit, I do not wish to mortgage or lease my planet, not for your jewel or for anything. Do you understand?"

The salesman paused for a moment, considering all the angles. "Kid, you are one tough bargain hunter. I will give you that, you get my hopes up, then you crash me down. Classic Low Ball selling, and I respect you for that, I do! Tell you what I will do, just for you, and because I like you: Let's say 30% off, and that's it, can't go any lower, yes?"

The boy just continued looking at the salesman, arms folded in that classic "no deal' stance.

"Ok kid. I've been hard up in the past. I know how it feels. Life can be that way sometimes, but there is something here that you can afford. It's a little memento, a way to remember our meeting with fond recollections in your old age."

With this comment, he digs deep into a side pocket of his pants and he pulls out a dull looking rock. "I had almost forgotten about this little rock I had here. It isn't much but it's a nice rock. It's something I think you can appreciate, and you can have it cheap, OK?"

With this he placed a small stone into the child's palm. It seemed like a rough semi-precious stone, maybe a chunk of old garnet, but it had an immediate effect upon my friend. He was instantly intrigued, and felt the rock all over then put it to his cheek, and then to his ear. "Hello" he said, as if speaking to an old well loved friend.

Ignoring the salesman, he took out the special lens that the Gardener gave to him in order to read the riddle about the butterfly, and then it happened. The boy's eyes lit up. "My aren't you beautiful!" he exclaimed in wonder. And lost to the discovery, he just gazed into that simple stone as if it were a treasure.

"I can see you've got taste kid, and the good news is that your good taste is extremely affordable today, and this little beauty won't cost you much at all."

The harsh reminder of money brought a sigh to the child. "I am afraid I just do not have any money," he said, flatly, putting down the eye glass. With great sadness he was getting ready to hand back his treasure.

"Wait a minute!" I said. "There may be something you might prefer to money, Mr Salesman." and with this I pulled out the piece of amber that my little friend had polished up. "Perhaps you might like to swap your old dull stone for this shining new piece of amber that was only discovered and polished 2 days ago." I offered the amber in my outstretched hand.

The man held it up to the light, and inspected it carefully. He ummed and ahhed for a bit, then finally said. "OK kid. You got a deal. I will take your worthless little chunk of amber and swap it for that priceless gem you now hold, and believe me you are getting the better end of this deal."

The boy nodded brightly, not believing his good fortune. "It's a deal!" he said.

"Sure thing kid. but hey, call me when you want to go upmarket, yeah?" And with these parting words the salesman simply dipped his hat, bowed low, and disappeared.

I am not sure where he went, or even how he came to be here in order to be able to vanish, but after a few days of the child's extraordinary tales it seemed to me that in this place almost anything was no possible. I was almost pinching myself to see if I were asleep.

"Thank you. Thank you so much for your kindness and generosity. I can never hope to repay you!" he said.

"But you are the one that polished the amber. I just picked it up. And anyway, you have already given me your wonderful stories and your company. That's worth more than money." I replied. "And besides, we can go to the forest at any time and find more amber but whatever it is about that rock he gave you, I could see how special it was for you in your eyes. Whatever it is, just to see you so happy is worth more than 10 pieces of that amber we swapped.

"But I am curious and would like to know: You refused a beautiful 3 carat diamond because it was not good enough, but this simple rock gives you the deep delight you have been looking for. What do you see in this rock that makes it so beautiful to you?"

He grew serious again, saying "It has an inner light, and it spoke to me. I don't understand her language yet, but I hear her inside. That's why I tried the Gardener's eyepiece, to see if it would translate her voice, and it DID!

"The diamond had beauty, but it was a beauty that depended on a reflection. Without an inner light what joy will it be able to give me in my darkness? We see a diamond in bright sunlight and it dances for us, but in the dark of night, what then? Those black rays of loneliness from my heart will dance there as easily as the light. This jewel is different. It has its own inner fire, and it warms me. I know that when I am sad it will not reflect my ugliness, but show me a better way. I know I can trust it.

He paused and looked at me. "I understand now, most people want the big things, things that are important to them. They want the big love that takes over their world, the big impression, the big home, but bigness on its own is very empty without the small things to fill it with joy.

"My Rose was a small thing that grew, and so was my love for her. It was small, but it grew. When I met the Gardener he showed me how that the emptiness I felt for her loss was really the seed of something greater.

"Here I was, looking for some great purpose and meaning in my life, but really my purpose was looking for a meaning in ME. But how to find this? Piece by piece my journey gave me the steps to myself, gave me the ladder to my Soul. And here I come to the end of the road and I find the Jewel that I didn't even know I had sought for so long. This is the place where my Soul has found a home."

Holding up his jewel he said, "My little stone is small and insignificant, like me, but I can feel its heart is true. Now I begin to understand why my Rose died, because if she had not left I would never have shed my tear, never made the rainbow, and never taken the journey to find out. Her loss was a gift I never recognised until now."

He handed me his stone, so I could look with my eyepiece, and I had to look several times to be sure. Yes, I was certain now. What I had thought to be a common piece of garnet has turned out to be something more far more rare. It was an exquisite uncut ruby.

He must have seen my eyes widen, because he laughed "Oh, so you see her too? She is a beautiful soul this one, isn't she." He handed me the gardener's looking glass as he spoke, and somewhat dumbfounded I took it and looked. And when I looked, I saw a soft ruby light suffused around the form of the stone, and I swear it spoke to me.

It didn't speak in words, but in a feeling. My heart felt warm, my mind cleared, and my whole being soaked in a sense of delight just having it in my hand. It was as familiar as a kiss on the lips from a lover of a thousand year, and yet it was a complete unknown. It was truly extraordinary, but how did he know?

The child knew it was a special stone the moment he saw it. "How did you know that you held a valuable Ruby and not just a common stone?" I asked.

"It told me" was all he said.

In that moment I knew something: I knew what I was missing in my life. I began to think of the emptiness of the office, the loneliness of my flat, the separation I felt with most people, and I sighed the saddest, longest sigh.

The child felt it, and asked, "Why are you so sad?"

"Well, out here in the forest everything is simple," I answered. "But soon I must go back to my life where rent must be paid, people must be spoken to who I don't really like, and things must be done that give me no joy. I am very happy for you, but it has shown me my own lack."

He looked at me for a long time, no words were spoken. The moon, though past full, was still bright in the sky. The lake still gleamed with a thousand sparkles. The trees still whispered in the dark. He just indicated to his Ruby, which I still held, and I knew he wanted me to look into it, which I did. And that's when it happened.

I felt it at first, the grass under my feet and the breeze just seemed to feel alive. I felt this life flowing up, like the heat of the sun, yet from the earth. The moon flowed into me, the lake flowed into me. The whole forest started speaking to my soul. It connected with me in a way I cannot find words to express, and as the energy of life slowly moved through my body I felt it touch every single cell. Speaking to me, connecting me to something must greater than myself, was an essence far greater than I had ever imagined.

It was then that I went flying. As the vibration of life moved like warm honey through the tips of my fingers and out the top of my head, I felt myself disconnect from everything I had ever been, imagined or dreamed. I was no longer aware of the limitations of my body, but free to roam the universe. And then I was standing in truth, reality, forever-ness. I was standing in that place where the Ruby existed, only in this place "I" was the Ruby itself.

I was the seed of life, the fire that burned with all truth, and I knew that I need not struggle. All I need do is to allow myself to grow. That's all I needed, to simply allow myself to grow. Tears flowed, pent up pain from a thousand lifetimes let go and left me free of the suffering. I was in the place where I needed to be. I had always been here, and all I ever had to do was simply to realise it.

The Return

I think I vaguely recall leaving the woods. I don't remember packing up and coming home, but I must have. I have no recollection of driving, or arriving. I just don't recall much else besides waking up in my bed feeling very, very different.

I got up and made some coffee, feeling somewhat confused. Had it been a dream? Yet when I looked over I saw the camping gear leaning against the wall, still unpacked from the journey. Or was it unpacked because this was all a dream, and I never made the journey? Who was that child?

I looked about, and obviously he was not here in my flat, though I had half-hoped he might have been. I realised he had gone back to whatever planet he came from, and that I would never see him again. I felt an enormous piece of my heart missing in that moment, a real emptiness. Surely his wonderful stories were with still me, but that was all.

Lost in the world of contemplation, sipping my fresh brewed coffee, my eyes fell onto a small book that was open on the table, with the words from T S Elliot.

It was the strangest thing. I had never read this poem in its entirety before, that I could recall, at least. I had gotten the book from the library so I could look up for the quote I had remembered: "Come back to the place from whence I first began". To my surprise, reading it before I fell asleep I found that this quote was not in the poem at all, and awake now, I could see how so much of the story of the child seemed to be entwined into it. It seemed far more than mere coincidence. Had this poem triggered a lucid dream?

T. S. Eliot, Four Quartets, Section V

With the Drawing of this Love
And the voice of this Calling
We shall not cease from exploration
And the end of all our exploring
Will be to arrive where we started
And to know the place for the first time
Through the unknown, remembered gate
When the last of earth left to discover
Is that which was the beginning:
At the source of the longest river
The voice of the hidden waterfall
And the children in the Apple tree
Not known because not looked for
But heard, half heard in the stillness
Between two waves of the sea.
Quick, now, here, now, always –
A condition of complete simplicity
(Costing not less than everything)
And all shall be well, and
All manner of things shall be well
When the tongues of flame are in-folded
Into the crowned knot of fire
And the fire and the rose are one

I looked out my window at Barnclueth Square, and down onto the park below. Kings Cross and the sound of Sunday in Sydney came up to greet me. Children played with other siblings, alcoholics slept under newspapers, the Winter Sun spoke to the green of leaf and tree, and the never ending traffic buzzed like an alarm. It all seemed so normal, and yet so completely strange.

It was difficult for me to connect the dots between where I had been in the forest and where I was now. It was confusing. Was it real, or a dream?

Yet if I closed my eyes, the image of the lake became crystal clear in my thoughts. I could touch it, smell it, and I would swear that if I turned around, there I would be, back in the forest. But when I looked about it was just my flat, with worn carpet and persimmon coloured walls. The water bed rippled as if someone had just sat on it, and a breeze blew through the window. The only thought I held in my mind was the title to the Robert Heinlein book "Stranger in a Strange Land". It occurred to me: Was this really my world? Am I simply visiting as well?

A distant hum calling me to action rang in my ears. It was that familiar ring of inspiration which all writers know, that bell toll of something that would trigger the creative soul within. Looking over I see my old Remington that sat on the kitchen divider, sheet in roller, ready for work. I knew this passing breeze had to be caught before it faded into nothing. As always, I sit down, and wait. This was when the short prose called "The Lake" fell out onto the typed page.

The Lake:

I am the lake. For so long have I existed that time itself is but a memory. The future is a dream, the past is done. There is only Now. I exist within myself, for myself, by myself and though many may come to visit my shores, few there are that know me.

In silence I abide, awaiting the seasons that brush my face like a gentle breeze. Cycles flow like a never ending wheel where I am the pivot, the rim and the spokes. Do I count the many who come to quench their thirst from my waters? Not at all. A thousand, thousand have come, and still more I can see in the distance, but though they take what they will from me, the depth of my heart remains untouched.

My brim is ever full. Storms may come to taunt me, ice may freeze my surface, drought may lessen my being, yet beyond it all I am constant, ever present despite the changing landscape.

Young children, carefree and with boundless energy, throw rocks to see them skim and splash, and slowly these fall within to my heart. I absorb it with the deep water of being and take the rocks for what they are, the symbol of youth. Time will bring the children of men to understanding, and they will come back with their children, and their children's children, and with each age they will remember me.

With each age I will share a little of my peace with them, allow them to grow as they will. Perhaps they will grow into the harmony I give to all? Yet I know only the wisest of them will ever find more than an inch of the mile I offer. Always will my secret remain.

Animals come at eventide, all animosity of hunger set aside as they drink in my presence. Bowed heads, not in worship, but in acceptance of what I am, and where they must be to reach me. They kiss me with unspoken gratitude, and it is enough, for I know that by the gift of life I give them, that all of life will return, again and again to my shores, making the perfect circle.

By my gift of being others will live, and yet I will lose nothing from the gift. The river of life feeds me more than all of creation can take. Yet man, that sad dreamer, so often he forgets my balance, my simple way. He will chop down my friends, the trees, and use them to put up boxes he will live in. He will claim that he owns a piece of my shore. He would try to hold my essence, and tie me down with pieces of paper?

This is madness.

This child of creation is so young. He would seek to dam the river, to own life and nature, and try to say *"Look I have tamed the great river, I own the great lake, I am greater than all of creation!"* But time and season will wear him down. The earth will shake, the tides will change, the moon will look down and smile her ever present smile. In a moment of creation, but a day of eternity, his works will be washed away. Man's lifetime is but my moment, his civilization, but a single hour. The flood of change comes, and man cries out *"My God, why hast thou forsaken me!"* Yet I remain through it all, the reminder to man, to life, to all. A reminder of the greater peace that only the depths of being can bring.

Yes, I am the Lake. The waters of time must run to me no matter the plans of man, for this is how a river runs. Other men will fish from my waters and when they discover my worth to another with the food I give, greed overtakes and rules their hearts. One day, no fish are left, and I am cursed for failing their desires. But seasons come and greedy men go, and always there is a fish I have kept secret, so in time they return to swim in my waters.

Many will come on hot summer days to cool their weary bones, and I refuse them not. As they sit and admire the beauty I give, I feel their joy, yet I know there are precious few that will find the greater gifts I offer.

Through all the passing parade of experience, I remain.

I am the the Lake, silent and sure. Will you stop your frantic rush through the dream you call life, and truly ponder my depth? In my heart you will find a stillness that is alive with freedom, an abundance that is rich with emptiness, and a moment that lasts forever. Is this what you desire? Do you want this? Do you even ask how you can find this?

Just pause, just stop, just bow your head and recognise that where you are is not where I am. But within there is the place we share! Within, where your own waters flow. That place where your dreams sleep and await fruition, where all your hopes reside, and where your childlike joy abounds. Here I await you, but you do not see this.

Man likes to feel he is above creation. You have the freedom to roam, to come and go, to cherish or ignore me. You have so much choice that is becomes a burden for you. You are gifted with intelligence and feeling, yet what joy does it bring you? Yes, you are above me, yet stop and imagine what it would be like if I were to put myself above you? You would drown, dear soul, in my presence.

I am ever at your feet. I am the Ocean of Being. I am an abundance only dreamed of by poets. In my quiet all there is temperance. I have patience enough to withstand the greatest of evil, and know that your evil will be suffocated in my presence. And be warned, if you hold to that which harms life, you in turn shall be drowned.

I am the lake. I am the sum total of my drops yet never more than a single one. Each drop holds everything I am, and so if you but drink from me once, you receive all I have to give. Stop! Gaze deeply into my heart, sad dreamer, I welcome you.

I am the Lake. I am that depth of being within you. I am the eternal waters you seek.

Fear not change. Change is the way of things. All storms in life are but movements in the greater flow of things. Let go of that which troubles you, that which wrinkles your brow. Know this: Within your present truth one thing is certain, a greater vision awaits you. Whatever you presently behold, there is a greater love you can find. Just let go! Stop fearing I will drown you. It far easier to let go, to let slip away the moments of turmoil and strife. In your true depth, they will all become but ripples on the surface of your being.

I am the Lake. I have always been the Lake, and though you tarry long within your dreams, here I shall remain: Neither high nor low, neither great nor small, and never am I more than this moment within which I dwell.

I am the Lake. I shall always reflect to you your truth. Even as I accept you for what you are, I will show you exactly what this may be. Just stop and gaze into my heart and allow the mirror of my being to show you yourself. But beware! Beware of Narcissus, lest he seek to own you.

I am the Lake. My ways need not be observed, my path you cannot follow, and yet my truth cannot be denied. You may find my simplicity complex, yet I find your complexity simple.

I am the Lake. I will exist whether you deny your thirst or sate it. I will remain whether you lie parched in the desert of loneliness or come to my shore and bath in the succour of my serenity. Should you just bow down to receive, you shall receive. Kiss my wisdom with your lips and you shall be sufficed, and I will delight in softening your hard, dry countenance with my being.

I am the Lake. I am ever at thy feet, and care not if you recognise my great depth. You have feet to travel, and you may travel far, yet only when you are still like myself will you know the ending of your journey. Be still, look into my heart, and I promise you that you will see deeper into your own. The only question that remains: Will you bow down in order to receive me into your being?

Can you be humble enough to be free?

Author's Note

This book is not Tolstoy, nor does it seek to be. It is a simple tale from a simple time. When it was written I was not well, and indeed, I was on death's door. Weighing just over 7 stone and wearing girls 24" jeans I looked like I lived on another planet. Most people imagined that I must have been a drug addict. I was addicted, in a sense. I needed desperately to possess freedom, and truth. So much so that I didn't really notice how thin I looked in the mirror.

But I knew that barely eating food for almost 2 years was not a recipe for a long life. Eventually I got past the health issues, and in looking back I realise it was the writing that kept me alive.

Writing words like this book were my food. The act of creation is what kept me going. It gave me purpose in an otherwise meaningless existence. Now, 37 years later I finally publish this book. Perhaps it will give you a hint of something I desperately needed back then: A genuine sense of self-worth.

I did take that journey to the wilderness, and I cannot remember in detail exactly how it happened, or when it happened, but I have the handwritten copy of a book that I wrote during that period to prove it did. But otherwise I was so near to death and thus so far away from this world that I barely remember anything but snippets of those months. All I know clearly is that after 6 weeks on water, and another 6 weeks on fruit, that I came to understand an extremely simple truth: "It's only me." (This theme is taken up in a later book, Jerimiah Versus the Grabblesnatch)

By recognising it was just me, I accepted myself, and stopped needing to be important to others. This simple understanding is what freed me from my own prison and allowed me to start cooperating with life, rather than seeking to be "above it" in some way. By accepting myself as I am, I no longer needed to defeat the opinions of others with ever greater opinions, or demonstrate I was "better" with some type of success.

Many years later I was to discover that these were the exact words John Lennon spoke to the other Beatles when they got into arguments. "It's only me." John Lennon would say to his friends when things got heated. It's a great leveller, and this simple thought has sustained me all these years.

I trust you will have found something in these pages that will help sustain you on your journey.

Michael Wallace

22 Jan 2015

PS: A most curious thing. 20 years after I wrote this book, I bought a property that had a small lake, with a waterfall. It was at this place that I raised my young son.

Now, this happened some years before I discovered the original manuscript for "Hello Planet Earth" in the storage box I had collected from my sister's warehouse, yet many of the journeys and stories in this book were echoed in what I tried to teach him. Indeed, it would seem I had arrived at where I started.

A part of this story is recounted in another book by myself (written in three days) called the Boringbar War. (Available on Amazon)

The Small Lake and Waterfall at the property
where the "Boringbar War" was set

have no companion but Love, no beginning, no
end, no dawn. The Soul calls from within me:

"You, ignorant of the way of Love! Set Me free."

Rumi

Fragments of the Mirror

Author: Michael Wallace

Available on Amazon

If you loved "Hello Planet Earth" then please go to Amazon and buy "Fragments of the Mirror". These are short stories that came from a similar period in the authors life, and have the same sweet resonance that restores kindness and love to the heart.

Alternatively: go to laddertothemoon.com.au and follow the links

An almost biography written in three days

Being a tale of madness mayhem and mystery mingled with martyrs, maids and myopic miscreants

The Boringbar War

Being a Tale of the War
and the Pieces Left Behind

Michael Wallace

"This is s really remarkable achievement. A wonderfully entertaining, and very original writer"
Professor George Cockroft
(The Diceman)

The Boringbar War

Author: Michael Wallace

Available on Amazon

This is a truly remarkable novel. Written in just three days in June 2005 as part of the Three Day Novel Race, the author catapults the reader through as extraordinary (apparently) true tale of madness, mayhem and mindless destruction.

"A really extraordinary achievement" wrote Prof. George Cockcroft, writer of "The Diceman"

Available on Amazon. Alternatively: go to laddertothemoon.com.au

Are you ready for something different?

From the same writer, we bring you the Divinity Dice Series. This series introduces a series of games that cast dice to give clear answers to questions you ask. It is remarkably accurate, and part of the Pythagorean Tradition made available for the modern person.

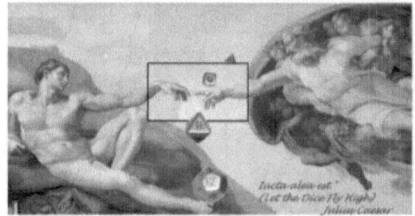

DIVINITY DICE

Play the Dice of the Gods

Cast the Dice of the Gods and allow Life to give you the answers to your deepest, most secret questions

Iacta alea est.
(Let the Dice Fly High)
Julius Caesar

Author: Michael Wallace

Play the Game of Life

Have Fun with Divinity Dice and discover amazing answers to your deepest questions. Discover how the Ancient Art of Prophecy is still alive in the 21st Century. The Greatest Secret is in Your Hands Right Now!

Divinity Dice is produced under the authority and auspices of the Pythagorean Guild.

These books were written to help the individual grasp how number combinations worked. They provide an easy, practical way to give a natural "Oracular" readings, based on the various castings of the polyhedral dice.

Go to divinitydice.com.au for more information and pricing.

There is also a series of fun workshops available, which allow an individual to grasp the power of the Dice in a group atmosphere.

Absolutely ground breaking stuff!

Without doubt, the most comprehensive books on Dice Divination on the planet.
George Cockcroft, writer of "The Diceman"

Michael Wallace (Raven)

Michael Wallace is a remarkable individual. He is a Master Musician, Master Body Worker, Master Numerologist, Dice Master, Recording Artist, Songwriter, and Publisher. On top of all this he is also a prolific writer with over seventeen titles in print.

Known as "Raven", or what the Hopi describe as the Storm Bringer, he is a catalyst for change and renewal.

The Book of Number Series

Available on Amazon

Have you ever felt that there was something more?

The ancient art of Divination by Number is an extraordinary study you may wish to contemplate. The author of this book has written a complete course on "how to do" Pythagorean Numerology. In just WEEKS you can learn to discover and understand all the numerical secrets of the Ancient Greeks.

The Book of Number is a series of four books that cover the whole teaching of Number Divination as taught by the Ancient Pythagoreans. This is, available on Amazon or direct from the author. Details are below if you wish to know more.

www.bookofnumber.com.au

For further enquiries and updates go to the official web page at bookofnumber.com.au.

You may also write to info.numberharmonics@gmail.com.

Here you will find all current information on Pythagorean Numerology, as well as where you can find study groups, on line classes and areas of interest to the subject.

RATOLOGY: Way of the Un-Dammed

By the same author. Available of Amazon. An extraordinary insight into what drives people, and discovering the simple ways how you can take charge of yourself.

Jerimiah Versus the Grabblesnatch

By the same author. A modern myth, in a similar vein to "Hello Planet Earth". Available through laddertothemoon.com.au

www.ingramcontent.com/pod-product-compliance
Lightning Source LLC
Chambersburg PA
CBHW032121020726
47494CB00007BA/2180